CHRISTMAS MURDER OF A MISER

Historical Cozy Mystery

ANDREA KRESS

© 2022

Created with Vellum

Chapter 1

I had been married less than a month and marveled that, despite the momentous rite of passage, I still felt like Aggie Burnside, young nurse, although obviously I was now Aggie Taylor, young nurse and doctor's wife. I still worked for my doctor husband, John, in the two medical offices, one in nearby Adams and the other located in our home in West Adams. It did feel a bit strange to refer to almost everything using the possessive 'our,' but according to our vows and all the legal documents I had recently signed, it was true.

Our work schedule had not changed: mornings in the modern Adams office in the Professional Building on the main street in town and afternoons in the homier suite of rooms just through a door from our private kitchen. The one big change had been that I no longer lived in Miss Manley's house catercorner to us nor did I get to take advantage of the wholesome country meals prepared by Annie, her housekeeper and cook. However, we kept up our close relationship by alternating Sunday dinners first at her house then at mine, although my culinary skills were still in their infancy. One thing that had not changed was my attendance at her weekly tea group gathering, an old-fashioned affair where everyone was addressed as Mrs. or Miss, this being a women-only group, with information and gossip shared in equal measure.

Another change was my routine at the end of a workday. No longer did I wander through the kitchen of Miss Manley's kitchen, inhaling the aromas of the dinner being prepared before leisurely going to my room and kicking off my shoes. If I had wanted to put my feet up or dash off a letter to a friend back home, there was plenty of time to change my clothes before dinner. After the first few days together in my new residence, it seemed our pace had quickened and, once the office was closed at the end of the day, we were in the house, quickly changing into casual clothes and going back downstairs to prepare dinner. We stopped and looked at each other in wonder.

"What are we hurrying for?" John asked me.

I laughed and fell into his arms for his warm embrace.

"We've got some of that bootleg hooch in the pantry. I propose we have a proper cocktail hour each day after work," he said.

"That's an excellent idea. I believe we have some cheese and crackers. We are so very sophisticated," I added.

John lit the fire that had been laid, and we settled in the sitting room to review our day.

No sooner had he taken the first sip of what we called our country martini than the telephone rang. He put his hand through his hair and grimaced in my direction, expecting some emergency call, but after saying hello, he broke out in a broad smile.

"Cash! How nice to hear from you." He looked at me in surprise. People didn't just call long distance for idle chat, but then, he was one of the few people of our acquaintance who could afford it since he had made a fortune several times over from his various businesses.

I stood up and put my ear next to the receiver John held in order to hear the conversation.

"And we can't thank you enough for your most generous wedding present," John said, referring to the automobile he had gifted us.

"You deserve it for your practice," Cash said in his booming voice. "I wanted to tell you that I have been trying out a new diet regime and it's working wonders."

John gave a wry glance at me, wondering what strange experiment Cash was trying out this time since he liked to consider himself a modern man constantly adapting to the times or being ahead of them.

There was a long piece about avoiding certain vegetables in favor of others, drinking beef broth and eating smaller meals but more of them. It didn't sound injurious, just a lot of trouble for whomever was preparing his food. But, for a wealthy man with a full-time chef and plenty of staff, that would not present a problem.

"Oh, and another thing," Cash said, chuckling. "I wanted to tell you a certain reptile is reported to be in your area soon."

My eyes widened at that statement. I had only seen garter snakes and that was rarely. The last thing I wanted to do was to be hyper-vigilant on my walks through the woods or give them up altogether in favor of town strolls.

"What do you mean?" John asked in alarm.

"A certain Theodore Schaeffer has put a bid in on Highfields and my reliable sources tell me that not only has it been accepted, but he'll be in your neighborhood soon enough."

"That was fast," John said. "I mean, after it's sitting idle and being rented and then unoccupied again. Did he tell you himself?"

Cash let out his big laugh. "After some nefarious things he tried to pull on me, we aren't exactly friends. But I do know a reporter from the **Knickerbocker News**—I know, I know, not a very reputable paper in New York—still, it pays to have eyes and ears everywhere. Schaeffer bought the mansion lock, stock and barrel. Furniture and everything."

"Wow!" was all John could manage to say.

"And now that everyone knows he's trying to sneak out of town under cover of darkness to avoid any number of lawsuits and ex-wives out to put the squeeze on him, you might expect to see some new faces in town. Including said reporter, looking for additional dirt on Schaeffer to sell more papers." He chuckled.

"Things have been a bit slow here lately, but I don't know if we were expecting an increase in population anytime soon."

"Just don't get caught in the crossfire. Watch out for Schaeffer, and don't say I didn't warn you."

Chapter 2

That cast a pall on our jolly cocktail hour, wondering what we could expect from our new neighbors up on the hill who had the best view of Mount Greylock and the valley below. And why did Cash think it was going to have anything to do with us?

"Do you think we should lock up the silver?" John asked with a smile.

"Anyone who can afford to buy that huge place on what seems to be a whim, he's got plenty of silver already, I'm sure."

"I expect if he's anything like Cash with regard to being obsessive about his health, we may be seeing him as a regular patient."

"That wouldn't be so bad," I said. "At least he won't be paying you in single bills or change in an unmarked envelope shoved through the mail slot like some of our folks." That was not an exaggeration since I did the books and sometimes had to figure out from whom the payment was.

"I'll bet you it wasn't too long ago that people paid the doctor in eggs, cheese or ham," he said. "I wouldn't mind having a big ham hanging from a beam in the kitchen."

"I certainly would. And there aren't any exposed beams in the kitchen here unless you're thinking of us moving to a nearby farm. Speaking of ham, what were we going to have for dinner tonight?"

We had come to the unusual, but for me, quite agreeable decision, to divide up the cooking responsibilities—meaning that we decided on a menu for the week and rotated with one of us cooking while the other did the wash up. His long experience living alone and cooking for himself gave him more experience than I and he liked to boast that it was the reason I married him. I could tease him back by saying he married me to save himself from having to pay my nurse's salary. In reality, the money all went into the same pot now, so what did it matter?

Sitting down to a roast chicken, stuffing and squash, I reminded him that there were thank you notes to get out in the next few days to our local neighbors and friends for attending the reception that Miss Manley had hosted and the generous gifts they had given us, like the colorful platter in front of us.

"The tea group ladies really like and admire you," John said. "When you first came here, I thought they would regard you as some snobby, modern, city girl."

"That's me all right," I said, laughing.

"As down to earth and genuine as you are, people have preconceived notions, you know. I think the uniform really set the tone that you meant business. But in a good way."

"You're right. Uniforms tend to convey authority, which is why they are used so effectively. Do you think I should still wear it? Or is that a bit too stuffy?"

He pondered a moment. "While it might be all right to revert to your usual wardrobe here in West Adams where people know you, I still think the uniform is the proper look. First, it should impress the heck out of the Adams office patients in our new, spiffy location. And then, we wouldn't want people to think that we've lowered our standards. After all, I still wear my lab coat each day. How would it look if I showed up in a flannel shirt?"

"You would look like most of the men in this part of the world. But I agree. Uniform it is. I worked hard to earn that nurse's cap and I'm going to wear it. By the way, this chicken is excellent. It's making me think that we ought to put up a chicken coop when the weather warms up. Fresh eggs and fresh chicken."

"Aggie, you are getting ahead of yourself a bit. Someone must feed the animals, gather the eggs and then, are you ready to slaughter the dear little things for dinner?"

I made a face. "No, I couldn't do that. Maybe we should have rabbits instead."

"Pass the gravy, please," he said in response.

I giggled.

"What's so funny?"

"How you change the subject when you don't want to discuss it."

"Guilty as charged."

Although we had decided not to talk shop at the dinner table, it was inevitable as something would slip my mind or his during the course of the day. Thus began a discussion of an unusual proposal that had come from Doctor Schell, a surgeon working mostly out of Pittsfield. He wanted to make his practice more accessible to rural patients who often had a difficult time with transportation into the larger city, and he was aware that we only had the Adams office open in the morning. His idea, which seemed strange at first, was that he use that space during the afternoon hours when we were in West Adams.

The more we talked about it, the better the concept sounded. There would be little to no alteration of the space, which consisted of a reception area, one exam room and John's office. Doctor Schell could have his own file cabinet as there was plenty of room, and his name could easily be painted onto the upper glass portion of the door. The arrangement had advantages, too, in that if a potential patient just walked in expecting Doctor Taylor, they could be informed of his morning office hours instead of meeting a locked door. Better yet, from my practical way of thinking, the rent would be shared between them.

"I'm glad you have that head on your shoulders, Aggie. I know that in the past I didn't always make the wisest financial decisions."

"None of us do," I answered, thinking of a particular lilac hat purchase that I made in the City months earlier. What was it about women and hats? Every department store had an enormous area set aside displaying the latest headgear, each new design more fanciful than the last. Part of the blame went to women's magazines and movies where the actresses had extravagant concoctions on their heads. I considered myself lucky being able to ignore the issue since I wore my white cap each day and, except for attending church, I let my hair go uncovered.

We had just finished eating when the phone rang and John got up to get it, followed by a look of surprise as he spoke. I cleared the table, trying not to make too much clatter, but the conversation was soon over.

"That was Theodore Schaeffer," John said when he returned.

"Already? Did it seem to be an emergency?"

"No, although I assume he must be at Highfields since it wasn't a long-distance call. He wanted to have a preliminary discussion with me, as he put it."

"Not an exam?"

"He was terse, spoke rapidly and will stop by at the office here tomorrow afternoon."

We looked at one another trying to make out what this was all about.

"Where's your snake bite kit?" I asked, turning back to the sink to do the washing up.

THE NEXT MORNING before we went to Adams, I walked over to Miss Manley's to return a pie plate from Sunday dinner and saw Elsie, the former cook and maid of our other neighbors, the Lewises, sitting in the kitchen with Annie. She had effectively retired when she got married to Sam, a farmer and handyman, and her busy life seldom intersected with mine anymore. She looked happy and healthy and bursting with news.

"Sit down, have a coffee," Annie said to me, not waiting for my response.

"Just for a few minutes. We have to get going to the office. What's going on?"

"Oh, the commotion! Those people have moved in at Highfields. I should say they are in the midst of moving in, having hired any number of folks to unload trucks full of things," Annie said.

I sat down. "We heard that they had bought the house and the furnishings. What more could they possibly need in that huge house that's not already there?"

Annie shook her head and put a cup and saucer in front of me. She looked pointedly at Elsie.

"They are hiring people to work for them and somehow word got around, and they've asked me to be their chef, as they put it."

"Can you believe it?" Annie asked.

"Annie, I think you may need a change of title, too." That got a laugh out of both of them.

"What happened to your retirement to the farm?" I asked Elsie.

"Hah! Hardly a retirement. I've never worked so hard in my life! But once the harvest was in and the canning put up, most of the work is repairing fences and quilting for me and Sam's mother. Now things are slowing down along with the season, and I figured since it was offered to me, why not take it? I won't be living in, they've got some girls who will do the scullery work, and I couldn't say no to the extra money."

"Good for you!" I said.

"When spring comes and the farm comes back to life, I'll have to give it up, of course."

"Aggie, have you decided to move back in?" Miss Manley said from the doorway to the hall. Her smile was warm and there was a twinkle in her eye.

"I'm afraid John wouldn't allow that." The comment gave them a chuckle. "Just stopped in to return the pie plate and hear the latest gossip." I looked at my watch, took the last sip of coffee, thanked Annie, and said goodbye to them all. Just when I thought that West Adams was a sleepy little town, something like the Schaeffers' appearance got things stirred up. Now I was looking forward to meeting the man and wondered what his consultation would be about.

The morning in Adams informed us of the first case of what was probably measles, but the mother who called had the good sense not to drag her poor daughter through town and into the office, contaminating all in her wake. Instead, John agreed to pop in at their home just before lunch to make sure that the diagnosis was correct.

An older man came into the reception room coughing so hard that his face was bright red as he hung onto the doorknob. I immediately put on a surgical mask, asked him to sit and made a note to sanitize everything he touched when he had left. Just my appearance at the entrance to John's office in that attire gave him a clue of what lay ahead.

"Flu season," he announced, reaching into his desk drawer for a mask. "Let's get him in the exam room."

Another hacking session seized the man, but he managed to make his way to the room, holding onto each side of the door for support. I could almost envision the place teeming with germs but said nothing.

John did his usual exam and explained to the man that he was very lucky that he didn't have pneumonia and shouldn't have been out in the cold weather in his state.

"I know I have the grippe. Isn't there anything you can do for me?"

"I'm afraid not. You need to get in bed, stay warm, drink plenty of fluids, take aspirin to help with the fever and, for goodness' sake, don't be out and about where you could spread it to others."

The man thanked John and held his hand out to shake it, but John shook his head. "Stay away from other people as best you can. This is very contagious. And some people die from it."

He left with considerably more energy than he had come in with, and I carefully observed every surface he touched as he went out before filling a basin with water and bleach. Suited up in an apron and rubber gloves, I took a small towel, dunked it in the disinfectant, wrung it out and proceeded to wipe down all the places he had touched.

John nodded at my thorough approach until distracted by a phone call that he took in his office.

"This is going to be one heck of a winter," he said as I poured the remaining liquid down the drain in the sink. "It sounds like another case of measles." He stopped a moment. "You've had them, I assume."

"I'm surprised you never asked me before," I said. "Yes, I've had the lot: measles, German measles, mumps and chicken pox. Who hasn't?"

"This other poor girl, who happens to be best friends with the one I'm going to go see before lunch. Why don't I drop you off back home and do the rounds by myself?"

I remembered getting a house call from our doctor in Pelham when I was little and the flurry of tidying my mother created before his visit. I had lain in bed feeling miserable with the bedclothes perfectly arranged, as if any child could ever stay in such a position for any period of time. Not remembering what childhood disease I had at the time, my memory was that we were always instructed to be in a dimly lit room and be quiet. It was the height of boredom for a child and my brother was kept out in the event he would get sick, too, which he did anyway. The only distraction was an ancient bed tray that was taken out only for such occasions and the appearance of a book of paper dolls that I could cut from the cardboard and dress as they chatted with each other.

John dropped me off and I walked over to Miss Manley's since I had left so abruptly earlier. She was in the kitchen with Annie taking inventory of the pantry in preparation for a shopping trip.

"Hello, how nice to see you again!" she said, putting her notepad down and patting me on the arm. "Everything all right? You do smell of chlorine bleach," she said.

I laughed. "It's the newest scent from Paris, of course." I smelled my hands, which had been encased in rubber gloves, but I must have splashed some of the liquid on my uniform. I suspected that is why nurse's uniforms were white.

"No, just someone who seemed to be sick from the flu and decided to touch every surface in the office and exam room. Who knows how long those germs last?"

"Not very long with you on duty, I suspect," Annie said.

"Can you stay for lunch?" Miss Manley asked.

"John's making two house calls, so I'd better get something ready for him, but I wanted to know the report from Elsie so far."

Annie rolled her eyes. "She managed to get to the telephone and said the kitchen was well equipped, but they expected her to wear a chef's hat." She giggled.

"It's called a toque," Miss Manley supplied. "A good crossword clue answer."

"And she said that there are so many people coming and going bringing in boxes of papers and moving the furniture around as if there was something the matter with the way it was before."

"If they bought the house with the furnishings, I guess it's their business where things ought to go," I said.

"And a hospital bed. You know, one of those that you can crank into position," Annie added, hauling her hand around miming the action.

Miss Manley and I looked at each other. "I wonder who that is for?" she said.

"Elsie will call me again after work today and we'll find out," Annie said.

Chapter 3

I left them to their speculation and made my way across the backyard, then alongside the Lewises' house to ours, unlocking the reception room door and making my way to the door that led to our kitchen. I washed up and looked in the refrigerator and thought that a hot meal of hash and fried eggs would be just the thing.

I took off my cap and putting on an apron began to heat up the leftover beef and potatoes from the night before, humming to myself. I would eat my portion alone and reheat John's since he wasn't expected for a while yet.

I wondered if the hospital bed was for Mr. Schaeffer and if that was the reason he was coming to see John that afternoon. But if he could appear at the office, why would he need a special bed?

Once done with lunch, I set about to finish writing the thank you notes to the guests at Miss Manley's reception for us. We now owned a surprising amount of mismatched serving platters, a Foley food mill, a hand-crocheted Afghan in a bold blue color, bibelots, flower vases and several cookbooks. I wondered if the last items were typical for a new bride or if they knew I would need them. We had presented a unique situation for most guests because John already had a home and household set up and, unlike most brides, I had no need of dishes or glassware. I had read that in New York and Chicago some department stores encouraged newly engaged couples to register their preferences with them. In that way, wedding guests were relieved of the decision of what to purchase and, not coincidentally, the stores were no longer swamped with bridal gift returns after the wedding.

It was some time before John got back and he looked dispirited.

"Measles all right," he said, putting his bag down before washing up. "And the worst part is that the little girl is in a Brownie troop so we can expect more calls in the days to come."

"Have something to eat before someone else comes in," I said, lighting the burner to heat up the hash.

I sat with him as he ate and filled him in on the Highfields situation according to Annie.

"Mrs. Land, the girl's mother, wondered if someone from outside the community could have brought the infection in. I told her, of course, that was possible, but I didn't understand why she jumped to that conclusion. It turns out that her husband works in Adams and that the hotel owner mentioned to him that there were suddenly a lot of guests checking in from out of town. I guess she thought that was the origin of the infection."

"Is it so unusual for people to be in Adams at this time of year?" I asked.

"For early December? I should think so. 'Well-dressed city people' was the term she used."

"Ah, so was Cash Ridley's prediction correct?" I asked.

He shrugged and took his last bite as we heard the door from the street to the reception area open. "No rest for the wicked."

I put my cap in position and went out to greet a man whom I had never seen before.

"Schaeffer. I called about an appointment," he said abruptly.

He was about my height although very broadly built and stood with his legs apart as if in a fighting pose. He looked me up and down boldly.

So, this was the millionaire. He was a big man who looked as if he had just jumped off a boxcar in his rumpled clothes and his hat pushed back on his head.

"Please, sit down, the doctor will be with you in a minute." As I walked back to the kitchen, I could feel his eyes on my back, and it was not a pleasant sensation.

"Mr. Schaeffer is here," I announced and went back to my desk in reception. Our new patient had not sat down but was walking around the room, looking at the innocuous landscape paintings on the wall with some interest.

John came out and shook the man's hand and gestured for him to come into his office.

"No need. I sit down too much as it is. This your nurse?" he asked, jerking a thumb in my direction.

Well, I wasn't wearing a costume, if that's what he thought.

"I'll tell you why I'm here. My health is okay, but my wife's is not. I don't know what the heck is wrong with her, and the New York sawbones can't seem to figure it out, either. One of them thought the mountain air would help, so we bought the house up there on the hill. It was time to get out of the City anyway. She's in bed most of the day, and we've got enough staff to look in on her and one of them sleeps in an adjacent room at night. What I'm looking for is a private nurse to be with her a few hours a day."

He had addressed this entire speech to John although I was standing right there.

John looked at me and back to Mr. Schaeffer. "If you were interested in hiring Mrs. Taylor to be that private nurse, you might want to talk to her directly," John said pleasantly.

Mr. Schaeffer turned to me and said, "Well?"

"Well, what?" I answered with a question.

"Are you interested?"

"I think it would be a good idea for me to meet your wife first and determine what her needs are. Perhaps Doctor Taylor should have an examination of her, as well." I was flabbergasted at his blunt approach and had decided I should answer in kind.

He grunted. "I guess that sounds about right. Let's go."

"Right now?" John asked.

"I don't see any other patients," Schaeffer said, looking around the room.

"We tend to get walk-ins here in the country."

"How about after you close up shop tonight?"

He made it sound like we were running a restaurant and I had to suppress a smile.

"Let's say about five-thirty?" John asked.

"You know where we are. See you then." He stuck his broad hand out to shake John's, nodded to me and left.

When we were sure he was out of earshot, John shook his head and laughed. "I've never met anyone quite like that. When you think of a titan of industry or business giant, you think of someone like Cash Ridley—ambitious, sure, but also someone with style and class."

"How did Mr. Schaeffer make his money? It couldn't have been in the fashion industry."

"Now I wish I had asked Cash for more details when we spoke on the phone."

We had a slow afternoon, mostly people calling in about symptoms that sounded like the flu had made its annual appearance and would be here until early spring. I just hoped I wouldn't catch it.

Bundled up against the cold, we made our way in the dark early evening to the new car that Cash had gifted us. It was an extravagant present and my only regret was that we would reach Highfields before the heater could warm my legs. We approached the house lit up in a way that I had never seen before, as if every room was in use and we could see many figures moving behind the curtains.

"Gosh, that's a lot of activity. I wonder how many people are visiting?" I said.

John parked and after he rang the doorbell, it was answered by a young woman dressed as a maid in a black-and-white uniform. Compared to Mr. Schaeffer, she looked positively elegant. She had an old-fashioned headache band around her forehead, surely something from the last decade, although she seemed too young to have chosen that outfit for herself. I was taken by her hair, a short bob of a strange color brown that almost looked like a wig. Thick glasses completed her outfit.

She let us in and took us down the hall to the library and announced us to Mr. Schaeffer, who sat at the large desk puffing on a cigar. The room was practically blue with smoke, and I wondered if he meant to be off-putting for some reason.

"Glad you could make it," he said, standing up and smiling. Cigar smoking does nasty things to one's teeth and his were no exception. "Let's go upstairs."

"We knew the way, having been in the house many times thanks to the previous owner and subsequent tenants. He led us down the long upstairs hall where we passed two more maids who looked exactly like the one who had answered the door. I did a double take. Neither woman looked at us or at their employer, but continued in the other direction, as they carried linens.

Mrs. Schaeffer was installed in the feminine master bedroom with its white curtains and large bed, now pushed partly out of the way to accommodate the utilitarian hospital bed where she lay. She was dwarfed by the large contraption, and her pale complexion and blond hair almost blended into the white sheets.

"There she is," Mr. Schaeffer said, gesturing with the cigar still in his hand.

John introduced himself and me and asked if he could do a brief examination and ask her some questions. Mr. Schaeffer seemed to have lost interest in the conversation and left the room.

John asked if he could sit down next to the bed, which she kindly agreed to and motioned me to sit on the bench in front of the dainty vanity with its skirts of white material erupting from the kidney-shaped glass top. I was reminded about what an excellent bedside manner he had as he asked her questions about her health history, her stamina, her energy level, her mental state and if she was ambulatory. It was done in a calm, conversational way without him taking notes or reacting except with curiosity and follow-up questions. The gist of it was that she felt weak and lacked energy, but the doctors in New York could not definitively say what the matter was. She looked frail and delicate, but to my eyes not ill as such.

Then John asked if he could perform an initial examination taking the usual vital signs, which he did while speaking in a soothing voice. He asked her to stick out her tongue while he shone a light into her throat, felt the glands on either side of her neck, then took a thermometer out of his bag. While it 'cooked,' as we nurses referred to it, he took her pulse. He pulled down her lower lid then shone a light in each eye, used an otoscope to peer into each ear and fished around in his bag for the sphygmomanometer in preparation for taking her blood pressure. He asked if she was doing all right, and she smiled. Another conquest completed.

After a few minutes he extracted the thermometer, looked at it and nodded his head. While he was taking her blood pressure, I was looking around the room to see if there had been any changes since the original owners had left, but it looked much the same except for the hospital bed. It made me wonder why that was present if she was able to walk, as she had indicated. If she were habitually tired, she could just as easily have sat up in the big bed that used to have pride of place.

Then with a stethoscope he listened to her heart, her lungs, her breathing and asked if he could tap on her back and her stomach. There was a sharp rap that startled me and turned out to be a maid at the door.

"Excuse me, Doctor, but Mr. Schaeffer would like to have a word with you when you're done here."

"Certainly," he said, and she left.

"Thank you," Mrs. Schaeffer said to her retreating steps. Then to us she said, "I would have used her name, but I can't seem to tell any of those girls apart. Isn't that odd?"

"Have they been with you long?" John asked.

"We hired them in New York, and they seemed glad to be out of the City, although that's because Theodore offered them ridiculous salaries. That's how he gets his way."

"These days people feel lucky if they are employed," John said. "Well, Mrs. Schaeffer, what diagnosis has your New York physician given you?"

"One told me that I might be anemic and so I take an iron tonic. It's nasty and I suppose it does me good, but I haven't noticed a difference."

"Have you tried mild exercise?"

She stared at him.

"You said you were able to walk, didn't you?"

"Yes," she answered in a slightly suspicious tone.

"Did you ever take walks outside when you lived in the City?"

"Certainly not," she answered.

"It may be too cold or icy to walk outside at this time of year, but this is a big house. You need to get up and walk around and use your muscles; otherwise, they will atrophy. If you lie in bed all day, eventually you won't be able to walk easily."

Her eyes widened. "I never thought of it that way. I thought I was conserving my energy that way."

"That's true in some cases. But if you're otherwise in good health, as my preliminary examination indicates, you should be moving around, walking about the house, going up and down the stairs unless you are unsure of your balance." He smiled at her. "That is my prescription for the moment. If you think I ought to do more tests or take x-rays, we can do that, but I don't think it necessary at this time."

She looked perplexed. "Well, what should I do?"

He extended a hand to her, she took it and he helped her to her feet. She seemed a bit unsteady at first, but I thought it was less a physical reaction than surprise at being out of the bed. Her silk pajama bottoms were somewhat short, revealing slim ankles and tiny feet, but they managed to hold her upright as John let go of her hand. She laughed and took a few steps and then more toward me, smiling again, and then around the room until she lighted on the bed again.

"That was fun!" she said, color in her cheeks.

We were all smiles.

"I'd better meet with your husband now before we leave. Be sure to call me if you need anything or the exercise regime doesn't suit you."

John and I descended the staircase and, when I was sure no one could overhear, I said, "They're going to be calling you a miracle worker next."

"It might take a miracle. I can't tell without blood tests, but I think she may be suffering from either lung cancer or leukemia."

"Oh, no. The poor woman."

"Maybe her New York doctors didn't tell her, a practice I don't agree with. Perhaps she does know and chooses not to share that information."

"Not even her husband?"

"Who knows? All marriages are different."

A maid—again, I could not tell if she was the one we had just seen—stood at the bottom of the stairs and directed us to the study at the end of the hall. It still smelled strongly of cigar smoke, but Mr. Schaeffer seemed to have put it down for the time being. Better that than when men gnawed on the end. Horrible habit, in any case.

"Sit down, sit down. Well, what do you think?"

"Your wife's vital signs seem normal but her staying in bed all day does not seem to be a benefit at all. I neglected to ask her age."

"Hah! Guess!"

"Oh, no, you don't. I'm not going to get caught up in that conversation," John said with a smile.

"She's thirty-eight. Too young to give everything up, as far as I'm concerned. I've been married three times already and if she doesn't snap out of it, there will be a number four." He let out a huge guffaw.

"Now, really," John said with a slight frown.

"I mean it," Schaeffer said, pointing his finger at him. "Get her well or she gets out!"

"How do you propose that be done?" John asked.

"You, what's your name?" he asked, waving his hand in my direction.

"I'm Nurse Taylor," I said stiffly.

"For one thing, you come by every day for a few hours to encourage her to do something other than read. She needs to get out of bed. She needs to talk to somebody. This house is full of servants, most of them mute from what I have observed. Why don't you pop by between five and seven every day and have a chat with her. Cheer her up. Get her to do her wifely duty."

I'm sure my eyebrows raised at that last comment.

His eyes narrowed as he looked at me. "How about if I mention an hourly rate?"

"Go ahead," I said calmly.

He barked out a number. I tried not to react.

"Per hour," he amended.

I was very calm as I turned to John, who was trying to control himself. "Thank you for the offer. I'm sure you wouldn't mind if I discussed it with the doctor. The hours you propose are in addition to my full day's work but do not interfere with it. Still, I wouldn't like to have a negative impact on the practice."

"Sure, sure, sure. Have a chat. Talk it over. Give me a call. Then I'll see you tomorrow evening. Doc, send me your bill. We're going to make that gal well or…."

We thanked him and walked in shock toward the front door, where a maid stood ready to usher us out. I turned and saw what might have been her twin standing at the other end of the hall and wondered if they had mistakenly hired twins. The house was wisely built with a small foyer between the entrance to the hall and the actual exterior and we were hit with a blast of wind as we opened it to the night.

The car was at the base of the front steps, and it was as if by some silent agreement that we didn't speak about what just happened or what astronomical sum Mr. Schaeffer had proposed for my services.

It wasn't until we got back to our house, boots, gloves, hats and coats removed, that we both burst into laughter.

"Can you believe it? What is he thinking?" I said.

"Do you think you should take it?" John asked.

"You can't be serious! How could I not? It will be like babysitting except with an adult. Walking around the house, chatting for two hours—of course I'll take it."

"I don't like the man at all, and I don't like the way he alternately dismisses you and ogles you."

"I don't like him either. But even I do this for a few weeks, we could have that ski holiday in Stowe that you've been longing for."

John hugged me. "A real honeymoon," he said, kissing the top of my head.

Chapter 4

I duly appeared at Highfields the following afternoon about four-thirty, taking Glenda's car rather than walking because it was already getting dark. The house was lit up as the previous evening, and I parked in the back and went to the kitchen door where I knew Elsie would be working. Tapping on the glass, I let myself in to her big smile.

"Well, the whole town will be here soon," she said, before turning back to take a huge roast from the oven and heaving it onto the enormous six-burner stovetop. She poked at a large pot of potatoes boiling nearby then put the potholders back onto a hook next to the stove and gave a large sigh.

"That's a lot of food," I said.

"Sit down, sit down," she said.

I removed my coat and gloves and inhaled the deep aroma of the cooked meat as I perched on a stool by the butcherblock countertop in the middle of the room.

"The funny thing is, only Mr. Schaeffer has a full meal. His wife eats like a bird. Most of the food is for the servants. Can you imagine?"

"It seems like the medieval courts in Europe," I said.

"Eh? In what way?"

"So many people to feed at each meal, including the cooks who prepared all of it."

"These young girls have hearty appetites." She lowered her voice. "I don't know what any of them do during the day, but they are busy up and down the stairs carrying this and fetching that. I'm here in the kitchen all the time, but I can hear the footsteps up above. They don't seem to talk to one another, either, although maybe Mr. Schaeffer doesn't like chit chat."

"When do you get off for the day?" I asked.

"Five-thirty. So, we'll have some overlap."

"I'll be sure to come a bit early to keep you company."

"That's nice," she beamed. "Just before I go, I make up a tray for Mrs. Schaeffer. One of the girls brings it up to her and I have a feeling it comes back down half eaten." She shook her head at the waste.

The swinging door from the dining room opened and one of the maids began to walk in, but seeing me, hesitated.

"Don't mind me. I work here, too," I said.

She nodded and came into the kitchen and approached Elsie.

"The missus would like a pot of tea."

"Before dinner?" Elsie asked, peeved that her culinary efforts would go untouched if tea were served. "No food? Just the tea?"

"For now."

"I'm Aggie," I said, and the girl turned her face to me, her eyes enlarged by the lenses of her glasses.

"I'm Jane," she said, nodding her head. She turned and left the room.

"I thought that was June," Elsie said. "I'm glad I didn't try to do the introductions myself. I don't think I'm imagining that they look alike. Same hairstyle, glasses, stout body, and they never say enough that lets me identify them by voice." She gave a bit of a laugh. "I'm starting to sound like an old person," she said. "Maybe I'm the one who needs glasses."

She put the kettle on to boil and I told her I'd better go upstairs and see if Mrs. Schaeffer needed anything. I went through the swinging door to the dining room that could have easily held twenty people at table but only one place was set. There must be a servants' hall in the basement to accommodate everyone else although I had never been down there. The rooms on the first floor were quiet, and I could smell the nasty cigar smoke emanating from Mr. Schaeffer's study and wafting down the hall. I quietly ascended the stairs to the second floor and made my way down the corridor to Mrs. Schaeffer's bedroom. I knocked softly on the door and entered after she answered but was surprised to see a man in a three-piece suit seated next to her bed with papers in his hand. He seemed taken aback by my entrance and quickly put the papers into a briefcase at his feet.

"That's all for today, Robert," she said.

He nodded to her and to me and, without saying a word, left the room.

"Good evening," I said to her. "How are you feeling today?"

She sat up straighter in the bed and smoothed the coverlet with her hands. "I don't know what your husband did last night, but I feel so much more energetic today. I should say I had because this is the time of day when I feel like I'm fading away. I think the tea will revive me somewhat and perhaps I can eat some dinner."

I was puzzled for a few moments, wondering what it was I was supposed to be doing. I tidied her bedside table a bit then simply asked, "What would you like me to do?"

"Keep me company for a start."

Watch her drink tea and then watch her pick at a tray of food? This was the oddest job description.

"Would you like to play cards, or listen to the radio?" I asked.

"No, let's just talk."

"All right," I said.

"And please sit down."

I did and looked at her, hoping she would begin the conversation.

"How long have you lived here?" she asked me.

"I came up here a year ago in June when Doctor Taylor was looking for a part-time nurse. Not too long after that he took over another doctor's practice and my job became full-time."

"What are the people like here?"

"They're quite nice," I said and realized that was an insipid answer. "I thought that folks here would be less sophisticated than in the City, and in some ways they might be. But they are like people everywhere in their variety and have been welcoming and kind to me."

"That's good to hear. I hope when I'm better I can go out and meet some of them."

The bedroom door was ajar, and we heard one of the maids backing into the room with a tray with a teapot and one cup and saucer.

"Oh, no, Nan. You must bring another cup up for Nurse Taylor."

"I'm Beth, ma'am. I'll go fetch it."

I began to protest, thinking it was absurd to be paid to have tea with somebody, but she shooed my protests away. Whatever her illness, she must have been bored and lonely and why not have someone to keep her company?

"Do I get to ask questions, too?" I asked with a smile.

"Go right ahead," she said, enjoying the game.

"Why did you choose to move to the Berkshires?"

"Oh, I didn't make that decision. That was Ted's choice. He was tired of living in the City, and he said people were closing in on him. He had to get away."

Did she mean that there were too many people in the City or that there was some element of danger from which he was escaping? I didn't dare ask that question but went in a different direction.

"I'm sorry, I don't know if anyone told me what kind of business your husband has."

"He had many businesses. I don't even know if I could tell you what they were. He would buy a company that was in trouble, make it work better and then sell it at a profit. He's a very tough negotiator," she added.

I didn't think he was at all; there was no give and take in his offer of employment, he just assumed I would accept.

The door swung open, and the maid came in with a small tray with an empty cup and saucer on it that she handed to me.

"Thank you, Beth," Mrs. Schaeffer said.

"I'm Nan, ma'am. Would you like me to pour?"

"I'll let Nurse Taylor do the honors," she said, and the maid left the room.

"I was going to say that girls today all dress alike, but, of course, the maids wear the same uniform. Still, these girls all have the same hairstyle. And glasses."

"Did you hire them as matched pairs?" I asked.

That got a laugh from her. "I worked with an agency that assured me that they had excellent references. You know many wealthy families have had to cut back on expenses and that often means their live-in help."

It made me wonder again how Mr. Schaeffer had become so wealthy and survived in these difficult times to be able to afford that house and a stable of servants. And me.

"This tea is wonderful. It has a smoky taste to it."

"Yes, my favorite."

The conversation had come to a halt, and I tried to revive it. "Are there any family members who may be joining you for the holidays?"

"I don't have any children, and there aren't any from Ted's previous marriages, either." She looked over the rim of the teacup at me for a reaction, but I had already heard that information about the spouses. "Two other wives, can you believe it? Exhausting. For him and for them. In fact, I have it on good information that some of them have camped out nearby, hoping to squeeze more alimony from him. They think he moved to Massachusetts to avoid having to pay what was granted under New York law."

"Is that how it works?" I asked.

"I don't think so, but I wouldn't put it past him to pull a stunt like that. Are you shocked at my candid appraisal of my husband's virtues?"

"A little," I said tentatively.

"Let's hope you don't have to get to know him better. If and when you do, you'll find out he can be a real stinker. So why am I still married to him? Why not? I've given him some good years of my life, and I deserve to retire from the tiresome barbs directed at him that I endured living in the City. Comments in the newspaper, getting cut out of society functions, his carousing, the threats that came in anonymous phone calls and letters."

"That does sound frightening."

"None of it was aimed at me, but it still made going anywhere a living hell. Photographers camped outside our apartment building waiting for him or me to leave. I knew an excellent wigmaker—I used to be on Broadway—and he made me several different colored wigs that I used to disguise myself when I came and went."

I didn't know which thing to be more surprised about: that she used to be on Broadway or that she was harassed so much that she needed disguises to go about her day. No wonder she had taken to her bed.

"Those stories and more are for another day. If Ted doesn't do away with me before then. You've been here long enough, you can go now."

I looked at my watch. "I've only been here an hour," I said.

"I'm getting tired," she said, putting the cup and saucer on the nightstand and wriggling down under the covers.

I looked at my empty cup and wondered if someone had put something in the tea before moving the contents of the trays onto the vanity bench. She didn't move and I made my way quietly down to the first floor and encountered Mr. Schaeffer standing at the bottom of the stairs, effectively blocking my way forward. I stopped, excused myself to move past and he put his hand on my shoulder.

I turned abruptly. "Don't do that again."

He smiled and Cash was right, he did resemble a reptile. One with brownish bottom teeth.

"Of course, Nurse Taylor," he said with a smirk in his voice.

A maid was at the entrance to the dining room and had observed the interaction but did not react. I proceeded to the kitchen to fetch my coat, still disturbed by Mrs. Schaeffer's conversation and the behavior of her odious husband. It was entirely possible that he would fire me, and I wouldn't have minded in the least.

Chapter 5

John was surprised to see me return so early and I told him about the strange household and the revelatory monologue from Mrs. Schaeffer. I didn't relay the episode with Mr. Schaeffer for some reason.

He exhaled loudly. "It sounds ghastly. I'm sorry if you feel obligated to continue doing this job."

"Not sorry enough. Yet. I think she was just trying to shock me, or at least test me to see how far she could go with her narrative. It sounds like life in the City must have very unpleasant for both of them."

John poured me a small glass of wine that was a present from one of his patients and was surprisingly good.

"Let's go into the sitting room," he said.

I had taken off my cap but had not changed out of my uniform and was too weary from the day to do that yet. "She was vague about what kind of businesses her husband had but made it seem that he did a lot of buying and selling."

"Wheeler dealer, I think they call it. That environment can be nasty, and if someone thinks they've been taken advantage of, they'll scream bloody murder. Another factor, it seems to me, is that he comes from a rough background. 'Not our class,' as the snobs say. If he was interacting with the New York Old Guard, they would have expected him to play by certain rules. And I'm guessing he didn't."

"Mrs. Schaeffer said she had been on Broadway before they married."

His eyebrows went up. "Interesting. You'll have to get the details from her tomorrow."

"She said that because of her husband's reputation, she was shunned by society and they were hounded by the press."

"That could have been because of her background, too. Those toffs can be nasty if they think she was some kind of showgirl or gold digger. But I'm sure it had much more to do with his activities. After all, Cash called him a snake. I wonder how he was bitten in the past by the man."

"It was not very pleasant to hear," I said.

"I'm on KP duty tonight. I think we'll have the roast pork left over from the other night."

"Anything will do," I replied. "I'll finish my wine with dinner after I get out of these clothes." I couldn't wait to change into something more comfortable and put the gloomy thoughts out of my mind.

The master bedroom of our house was exactly like the room I had in Miss Manley's because she seemed to prefer a smaller front room that faced the street. I loved my room at her house with the big windows and a view of the back garden and the path that ran behind the houses. Here, I looked out on our dark back yard and side garden with the tall elm trees flanking the boundaries of the properties. It was more private and didn't afford me the comings and goings of the neighbors. Just as well, I had enough to think about now with two jobs. Or was it three?

The bit of wine I had consumed had taken the edge off my mood and as I was about to go back downstairs, the telephone rang. We had a phone in the kitchen and one in the upstairs hall, since John might be called in the middle of the night and nobody wants to scramble down the stairs in the dark.

"I'll get it!" I called out.

It was Glenda, a bit breathless but with excitement in her voice. She had been my classmate in nurses' training but hadn't graduated after the death of her mother, although she probably could have resumed her studies. She still owned the house in West Adams next to Miss Manley's, which she rented out from time to time, but she lived in Manhattan with her husband, Stuart, and their little boy, Douglas. We kept in touch regularly. I was the one who wrote letters, and she was the one who telephoned instead.

"How are things up there in the hinterlands?" she said with the bubble of a laugh beginning.

"Well, city slicker. Things are fine. I just have to go chop some wood and put the vittles on the table."

"You do not. I know for a fact that John does the cooking sometimes."

"My secret has been discovered!"

"I hope you are at least looking at the cookbooks that I got you for your shower."

"Why, did you want to read them yourself?" I teased. She was a totally disinterested housewife in that area.

"I want to know all about the Schaeffers buying Highfields. Why didn't you tell me?"

"We only found out the other day. There was quite a to-do as they moved themselves, a fleet of servants and truckloads of I don't know what."

"My spy told me that they had bought the house fully furnished."

"Your information is correct, and I can't imagine what they brought but Elsie got hired as their chef."

"What! When she married Sam, I thought she was going to be the farmer's wife. Hi-ho, the derry-o and all that."

"She did, too. But winter's the slack season and the new owners must have heard about her prowess in the kitchen. And I must say, they are extravagant in their wages. She couldn't refuse. Perhaps when it's lambing and calving season, she'll have to return to her former life."

"So, do you know about the Schaeffers?" she asked. And before I could answer yes or no, she launched into a vivid description of Theodore Schaeffer's reputation as a swindler who didn't play by the rules. What rules were those, anyway? But she emphasized that he had made so many business enemies in New York that he had virtually no more opportunities left.

"Except to live off the fortune he must have accumulated already," I said.

John came to the foot of the stairs and looked up inquiringly.

"It's Glenda," I mouthed, and he was relieved it wasn't an urgent medical matter to attend to and went back to the kitchen.

"I bet I know something you and your spy don't know," I said.

"What?"

"I'm working for a few hours a day as a private nurse to Mrs. Schaeffer."

That knocked the breath out of her. "Why didn't you tell me?"

"I'm telling you now. Today was my first shift up there."

"Is she really sick? What's the matter with her?" Glenda asked.

"Now you know I couldn't possibly comment on the health of a patient."

"I hate when you get all high and mighty with me. I'm sure someone will know and tell me. Let me guess: she's there for the pure mountain air, which means she drinks too much. Or she did something scandalous in the City and they had to make a run for it."

"I think their relocation has more to do with his activities. If no one wants to work with him anymore, he might as well leave. Bad press and gossip, as well. And he's left the state of New York, too. Put that in your pipe and smoke it." I loved to egg her on.

I could hear Stuart's voice in the background. "Glenda, who are you talking to?"

"Sorry, Barb, but I have to go. See you tomorrow." She hung up.

Barb was one of her new City friends and she didn't want Stuart to know she was making long-distance calls just to gossip. Perhaps by the time the telephone bill came in he would have imagined the call had something to do with her house in our town. I had to smile at her endless attempts to confuse her husband when it came to expenditures and glad that John and I didn't have that kind of relationship.

Chapter 6

It had snowed overnight, and everything was so quiet when we woke up as if a deep blanket had descended on the town, but it was only a light dusting. I could see the snow on the bare branches outside our bedroom window and gasped in delight.

"It'll be Christmas soon," I said.

John laughed at my enthusiasm. "We haven't even talked about whether to stay up here or go down to Pelham."

"And we'll have to get a tree. And we don't have any ornaments," I said with concern.

"That's what stringing popcorn and cranberries is all about," he said.

"I can see that you have never had to do that. The berries always squash, making a mess, and the popcorn hulls get in the way of the needle."

"Do we need a tree?"

"Of course!"

"We could have a tree without ornaments," he said with a smile.

"We could make those paper chains—remember making them in school? Small circles of colored paper linked together? And I know that there are some crocheted doilies in the bottom drawer of the dining room bureau. We could starch them and hang them up in the windows as if they were snowflakes."

By this time John had sat up, his hand holding up his head and he looked so happy at my silliness that I ruffled his hair and kissed him.

"The next thing you'll suggest is making those strange Nordic gnomes out of felt."

"Oh, yes! A high school friend of mine's mother was from Norway, and they were always on the mantlepiece."

"And when do you think you'll have time to do all this craft work and decorating? Next, you'll be outlining all the baking that needs to be done."

"Christmas cookies!" I don't know why I was so excited since it was still a few weeks away, but the notion that this was my house and my family now and we could create our own traditions was energizing. "How about fried eggs this morning?" I asked him, putting on my robe and slippers.

"Just make sure to put red and green sprinkles on top. We've got to keep this Christmas spirit going."

My good mood was in full swing as we drove to Adams, which had more cars parked on the street and in the road than I had ever seen before. John and I exchanged glances and were lucky to find a parking spot around the corner from the Professional Building.

"Perhaps the circus has come to town," he said.

We passed the owner of the café several doors down where we often got sandwiches for lunch, and he was in a tizzy.

"You won't believe it, but the Adams Hotel is packed to the gills."

"What's going on? A convention?"

"More like a swarm of angry bees. Someone got word out about the people up at Highfields and all these folks came up from New York to see about it."

"See what?" I asked. Were they there to gape at the house?

"I got the impression it has to do with the inhabitants." He shrugged and bustled off to work.

"They better not eat all the egg salad sandwiches in Adams. I have my heart set on one for lunch today," John said.

We were surprised to see that some of the newcomers were making their way up to our floor. While I would appreciate having the patients, I hoped they weren't bringing their own variety of flu with them—we expected to be struggling with more cases as the weather got colder and people stayed inside. Only one came to our door as we were about to unlock it, a man asking where he could find a dentist for a broken tooth. Luckily for him, Doctor English was just one floor away and he walked quickly toward the stairs.

I smiled at recognizing the New York City walk, very fast and intentional. People there were in a hurry and meant it. It probably also developed over time as pedestrians timed their pace to make every green light in a traffic-heavy environment. A group of three men and one woman headed for the attorneys' office at the end of the hall, all walking at the same pace. Good for them—the more business, the better, although it looked like serious legal issues were at stake.

"Oh, to be a fly on the wall there," I said. "Did it ever occur to you to be a lawyer?" I asked John.

"That seemed to be one of the two professions pushed in my direction. But I noticed that, while people may not get miraculously better after seeing a doctor, they almost always complain about having to see a lawyer, no matter the outcome. And then having to pay them. No thank you. Your father does well with his business law practice, but I could never imagine being in a courtroom situation. Too much tension and emotion."

"I think that was his initial intention and then realized he wanted the calmer existence of not bringing work home with him."

Our first patient came in and I had a hard time getting him to understand my questions about why he was there. He took off his flannel hat with the ear flaps but that didn't make communication any better. Then, reluctantly, he removed a wad of cotton from each ear.

"Earache," he said.

"Oh, dear. That must hurt in this cold weather. Please sit down and the doctor will be with you in a minute. If you'll just fill out this brief form," I added.

I told John about our walk-in, and he came out of his office, putting his white coat on over his suit. "Come into the exam room," he said, and I followed to make sure he had what he needed.

"How long has this been going on?"

"A few days. It hasn't got much worse, but it still won't go away. I put menthol oil on a cotton ball, but I don't know if that did any good," he said.

I could smell the menthol from where I stood and remembered how so many people swore by that remedy. John took his otoscope and peered into the ear.

"Yep, it's red all right. I'm going to put a bit of hydrogen peroxide in your ear, let it sit for a few minutes and then drain it out. Nurse Taylor will help you." By which he meant I would hold the small basin to catch the fluid.

Instead of complaining, the man giggled a bit when the liquid was squirted in. "Sounds a bit like fireworks going on in there," he said.

"Does it hurt?"

"No more than before."

We waited and finally John tilted the man's head to the side and let the ear drain.

"That's not really a cure," he said. "But it cleaned it out so things wouldn't get worse. I'd like to put more menthol on cotton in your ear, but before I do and you can't hear me, this is what I'd like you to do. First, keep your head well covered when you're outside. Then, when you get home, get a heating pad if you have one and lie down with your ear on it. If you don't have a heating pad, use a hot water bottle or a warm compress. Keep doing that until the pain lessens. And there is no shame in keeping your ears covered in this cold weather. All right?"

The man nodded and said in a loud voice, "My daughter will take good care of me."

He opened the door as a mailman I didn't recognize came in and handed us a stack of envelopes and two magazines.

"Where's our regular man?" I asked.

"Flu. They recruited me from Chester."

"Thank you," I said, thinking that the cases were coming on quickly this year. Shuffling through the pile of mail, I saw that one item was an alumni bulletin addressed to the young attorney down the hall. Since no patients were expected for a bit, I told John I'd be back in a minute and made my way down the hall, only to see him coming up the stairs from the floor below two steps at a time.

"This came for you," I said.

"Thanks," he said.

"Busy day in town," I said, hoping to get some information out of him. I'll be the first to admit, I was just being nosy.

"You said it! And here I thought December was going to be a slow month. That's what the partners told me. They said January was the busiest time."

"Why is that?"

"People putting off things until the New Year, making wills, starting lawsuits, that sort of thing. Thanks for this," he said and hustled down the hall.

That didn't tell me much but the Empire State license plates that lined the streets gave me the notion that, while things may have been brewing in New York, some people felt the need to hire a Massachusetts firm to represent them. Did this have to do with the Schaeffers?

I went back into our office and started sorting through the mail, carrying John's professional correspondence, bulletins and journals into his office and putting the weekly magazines out on the table and the bills and payments on my desk.

My concentration was disturbed by feet pounding down the hall and the same young attorney throwing the door open, alarm on his face.

"There's been an emergency! Someone fainted and she's unconscious! Come quickly!"

John had overheard the plea and rushed after him while I felt it best to stay and 'hold down the fort' as he always referred to it. I was dying of curiosity—was it one of the secretaries?

The answer came shortly thereafter when shuffling footsteps in the hall had me open the door to four men awkwardly carrying a woman whose arms and legs hung limply. They managed to get her into the exam room where I had already put the table in the supine position and place her on it. John asked the other men to stand aside while he loosened the top button of her suit and unwound the scarf beneath. Out of modesty, the three men retreated to the reception area and stood in shock.

John moved her head to one side, and we could see a huge lump forming on her temple although no blood was evident. "One of them said she was excited about something and stood up quickly, maybe too quickly, and either fainted or became dizzy and fell. That is some goose egg. That's a medical term," he added. "Can you get the ammonia inhalant?" He was referring to what most people called smelling salts.

They were at the back of one of the drawers since there was seldom a need for it, and scrabbling with my fingers past the instruments, I took it out and handed it to him. It was nasty stuff that for some reason Head Nurse Watson thought we first-year students in nurses' training needed to experience first-hand as practice patients.

John pulled his own head back, took off the top and wafted it back and forth under her nose until the desired effect of inhalation had her blinking her eyes and muttering, her hands fluttering in front of her face to push the offensive thing away.

"Ma'am, can you hear me?" John asked.

"Her name is Schaeffer," one of the attorneys in the reception area said. John and I exchanged glances.

"Mrs. Schaeffer? Can you hear me?"

She moaned and put her hand to the lump on her head and her eyes opened wide. "What on earth?"

"It appears you fell and hit your head," he said calmly.

"I think I'm going to be sick," she said, and I grabbed an emesis basin from the countertop and put it under her chin while John raised her upright. She retched, not producing anything, and managed to say, "Close that door!"

In our haste to deal with her, we had neglected to shut the door between the exam room and the reception area, and I apologized profusely. She glared at me, and John cranked the table so she was supported in a semi-upright position.

"Water," she commanded to no one in particular, which, of course, meant me.

She drank the water cautiously and touched the side of her head, wincing. "That was a very stupid thing to do." I thought she meant not closing the door, but she continued. "Hit my head on the edge of the desk, I imagine. What a day. What a week!"

"Are you traveling or staying in town?" John asked.

"At the hotel."

"Let's have you rest here until you feel yourself. There's no rush. Are you comfortable?"

"Can I get you anything?" I added.

She sighed. "No."

John went out to the reception area and told the men that she was resting for the time being and asked who was with her.

"I am. Elliott Johnstone." He shook John's hand. "Will she be all right?"

"I certainly hope so. That's a nasty lump and she may have a concussion. Is anyone staying with her?"

Mr. Johnstone looked uncomfortable. "I drove her up here this morning and we intended to stay until things got sorted out. But we have separate rooms, of course."

That addendum was the sure giveaway that they were more than friends or employer and chauffeur or however they classified their relationship. He sat down to wait, and the attorneys muttered their concern and returned to their offices down the hall.

"Can I get you anything?" I asked him.

"If you could get Ted Schaeffer off the planet sometime soon, I would be most appreciative."

My eyes widened.

"I'm sorry, that was entirely inappropriate. But no less heartfelt. You see, Marion and I would like to get married, but if we do, the alimony payments will cease. We won't have enough to live on with my investments gone up in smoke and my work precarious." He put his head in his hands and I stood there, not knowing if I was expected to respond.

"What sort of work do you do?"

"I'm in advertising. It was a great business until the world came crashing down in twenty-nine. I've had to do freelance work, which doesn't pay nearly as much as my former full-time job. And aside from doing the work, I've got to hustle every day to line up the next assignment. Money is tight as it is and if her settlement goes away, we'll be sunk."

John came out of the exam room. "If you'd like to go in…," he said. The despondent man got up as if the weight of the world were on his shoulders and made his way slowly into the exam room, shutting the door behind him.

John gave me a quizzical look.

Looking at my watch, I said, "I'll tell you on the way to West Adams later. We can't just leave her sitting in there. Do you think she might be able to walk with assistance and get back to the hotel?"

"We'll have to wait. I've got things to do," he motioned toward his office and went in, leaving the door open in the event he was needed again.

I went back to the bills and payments and could hear the couple talking in low tones. Finally, the door opened, and Mr. Johnstone came out and said to me that he thought Mrs. Schaeffer might be ready to leave.

"Doctor Taylor," I said, in case he hadn't heard the announcement, "do you think it is safe for the patient to get up and go?"

He sprang out of his chair, concerned that she might be rushing things, but saw that she was standing next to the exam table, her color was good, and she was trying to put her hair back in place.

"My hat? My coat?"

"I'll get them," Mr. Johnstone said and went quickly out the door and toward the attorneys' offices, returning with his coat on and hers over his arm. "Come, dear," he said, helping her into the sleeves of her fur coat. She didn't bother to put her hat on but carried it along with her handbag, her other hand in the crook of the man's arm, and they sailed out with as much dignity as they could muster.

Chapter 7

Doctor English dropped in shortly before lunch to thank me for the referral of the patient earlier and John came out of his office at the sound of the conversation.

"Doctor Taylor," he put his hand out for a handshake.

"John."

"Bob." He smiled and had perfectly aligned white teeth, as anyone would hope. He looked around the office and commented on how bright and inviting it was.

"Maybe I had better get rid of that ghastly pale green paint on my walls. I have a feeling there must have been leftover gallons in the basement somebody wanted to use up before it turned to stone."

"The maintenance man wanted to splash that on these walls, too, but I insisted on something a little brighter."

"Magazines—nice touch!" He picked up the latest **Saturday Evening Post** and flipped through the pages as if he were going to sit down and read it then and there. Realizing that he had been distracted momentarily, he said, "I can't tell you how many times I see men with broken teeth, not from barroom brawls—although I've seen that, too—but from gnashing them."

I smiled at the old-fashioned word.

"I mean grinding their teeth together out of aggravation or tension. That man was a prime example. He'd broken it down to the root, so I had to extract it. Gave him a bit of nitrous oxide and he was high as a kite."

Strictly speaking, he shouldn't have been discussing a patient with us, but often medical folks swapped stories, especially when it was something unusual. Bob English stood with his hands in the pockets of his dental smock and shook his head. "You would think with a mouth full of my hands and instruments he would have been quiet, but he had to tell me his tale of woe. And it was all Theodore Schaeffer's fault. As if I knew who he was talking about."

"He's the man who bought Highfields," John said.

"That place on the hill in West Adams?"

"The very one."

Bob whistled. "The way this man told the story, the only way Schaeffer ever got anything was from cheating people, and he drove all the way up from New York to confront him about it."

"Aside from clenching his jaw in anger, what was your patient intending to do?"

"I think his next stop was going to be the lawyers down the hall here. You know how businessmen are always suing one another. I could hardly understand what he was going on about, but he said that Schaeffer was going to pay." He looked at his wristwatch and said, "Got to get going, take care." His long strides took him out the door and we could hear him taking the steps two at a time.

"Whoever the patient was, he managed to shed some light on this convocation in Adams. Why all of a sudden are his enemies surfacing?" I wondered.

"Maybe he had better cover or protection in New York. His building must have had a doorman and here he is more exposed."

"There must be something else going on," I said. "We just met one ex-wife. I wonder if we'll see any others?"

∼

WHATEVER ALL THOSE folks were doing in Adams, they were not eating at the café down the street, and John got his egg salad sandwich that we brought back to the house. What I once thought was a nice luxury, I was beginning to consider an unnecessary expense. We could make our own sandwiches at home just as easily and save the cost. It might not amount to much, but I had become more conscious of every penny now that we were sharing our lives and I didn't have my own income anymore. Well, I did in one sense, but I didn't have a nice check to deposit in the bank each week, which had always been a satisfying experience.

The afternoon in Adams was a parade of sinus infections, colds, calls about possible additional measles cases and a woman with a nasty burn on her arm that was beginning to look infected. I watched the clock closely, not wanting to miss the weekly tea group, a source of female companionship, information and gossip. Promptly at four o'clock, I put my head into John's office and said, "I'm off."

"You're abandoning me to indulge in hearsay and delicious baked goods?"

"I'm afraid so. Then back to get the car and up to Highfields."

He gave an exaggerated sigh. "So, it must be. Give us a kiss, then."

I couldn't wait to see what Annie had baked for the afternoon event and I planned to sample each bar, cookie and tart. I was one of the first to arrive and helped Miss Manley lay out the treats, some on the sideboard and others on the low table in the middle of the seating arrangement.

"It has been so strange without you here," she said.

"I'm practically next door," I said.

"I know, but it's different when you came in from work and shared some of the events of the day. I get plenty of information from Annie, but it's not the same."

"Should I get unmarried, then?"

I liked to make Miss Manley laugh and she obliged. "Oh, you!"

Nina, Reverend Lewis's wife, also arrived early, her hair uncharacteristically mussed, but with a smile on her face.

"How is the baby?" I asked.

"Ellie is having a wonderful time helping her father sort out his notes for Sunday's sermon." She giggled. "I guess you've never seen his study when he is in the midst of organizing his thoughts. Scraps of paper all over the floor. Ellie couldn't decide whether to rearrange them or put them in her mouth."

"Ah, he's in charge this afternoon."

"Yes, and I'm glad you didn't ask if he were babysitting as if it were some part-time job. Mrs. Nelson has gone down to Hartford to see her daughter and he and I are covering all the bases in her absence."

"How lucky you are that he works from home most of the time. I was used to seeing my father only before and after his commute into the City for work. Weekends, too, of course."

"What's funny is that Robert never does baby talk with her. She never has a boo-boo when he's around. It's a 'minor injury' and it is not cured with a kiss but with a tiny gauze wrapping applied with a thorough explanation of the procedure."

"She'll be talking before you know it," Miss Manley said.

"She'll be reciting chapter and verse, most likely," Nina said with immense pride.

"When will Roger be home for the holidays?" I asked. Her nephew was attending Williams College and boarding there so, although it was not very far away, he seldom came home for the weekends. True to form, he was thoroughly enjoying the social life, the clubs and the mixers with the women's colleges nearby.

"He'll be back next week, I think. They have this strange schedule of a Christmas vacation and then return for a reading period followed by exams. Between exams and the next semester, they have a week off. I don't know what he intends to do during that time."

"Maybe the Mountain Aire will need some help with their winter guests who have come to the mountains to ski," I suggested.

"I think Roger is hoping one of his rich classmates will invite him to a winter home in Florida," she said. "Oh, the life of a college student!"

I smiled to think how Reverend Lewis had probably been nothing like that in college and Roger's parents were probably equally serious, serving as missionaries in China.

The other women came in and soon the teacups were filled, and the conversation rolled along. Mrs. Proctor, who had been serving as a County Commissioner, was all business as usual and not interested in light chatter and certainly none about babies.

"What do you all think about…" was the usual beginning of a sentence where you might expect that she was asking for your opinion, but you would be wrong. It was the jumping off point for a lesson in how she dealt with the 'big boys' and managed to maneuver around the obstruction of the red tape and the bureaucrats who she said were the real power behind the throne. I never did figure out who she thought was in the throne, however.

Miss Olsen had accepted a job as her assistant after having served as the unpaid volunteer during the lengthy campaign. Now, when asked what her job was, she would reply, "Whatever Mrs. Proctor needs."

Good answer, I thought, and it was not said facetiously. I thought the essence of her job was to make Mrs. Proctor look good, but that would not be the politic thing to say in front of her boss. Miss Olsen seemed to relish her job and it took her to Pittsfield each day, with its larger population, bustle and people to meet. Evidently, she got to meet quite a few young men and as a result, her social life had become busier.

Mrs. Rockmore had heard about the influx of people to Adams that morning and asked if anyone knew what was going on. I was quiet, waiting for someone to supply an answer and shortly, Miss Ballantine offered it up.

"Those people who bought Highfields have somehow stirred up a hornet's nest," she said.

"How so if they've never lived here before?" someone asked.

"I got the impression that they lived anonymously in New York City, it being so big and impersonal. Once they bought the house, someone let out the information and the pack came swarming up here." She nodded her head for emphasis.

"To do what?" Miss Manley asked.

"I know some of them were consulting lawyers to file suit," Miss Ballantine added.

I was surprised about how she knew that.

"Interesting. I wonder what it's all about," Miss Manley said, looking at me knowing that I was not about to reveal my involvement with the Schaeffers just yet.

"Have you heard about all the flu going around?" Mrs. Rockmore asked. "I'm scared to death my father will get sick with it. Terrible stuff." Then followed a recitation by each woman in turn of family members and friends who had died in the Spanish Flu epidemic in the late teens, though surely the current variety would not be so lethal.

"And now we've got the measles going around, too, haven't we?" said Miss Tierney, looking in my direction.

Of course, I could not name the patients, but I did nod my head at her remark. "Better to have them now than later," I said, sounding sage, knowing that it was dangerous for the fetus of pregnant women.

"I heard that Elsie was working up at Highfields," Mrs. Rockmore said, looking in Nina Lewis's direction.

"Yes, they hired her as a chef. A much more impressive title than what we gave her. And the pay was a steep increase, too. I'm glad for her."

"There are so many people up at that house! I was walking at the bottom of the hill and saw four young girls coming down the road, obviously maids although they had their coats on over the uniforms. Who has heard of such a thing here?" Mrs. Myers said.

I wondered why she was so surprised. Whoever lived there needed that level of help. Or was she surprised about the uniforms?

"They were chattering away but as soon as they saw me, they went quiet. I didn't realize I had that sort of effect on people." She laughed and we joined her, but knowing how formidable her stern-looking face could appear, I wasn't surprised that she had effected immediate silence.

I glanced at my watch and realized I needed to be going although loath to miss the rest of the gossip. It could wait. I excused myself and could feel curious eyes on me as I wound my way around the chairs in the crowded room and went to the kitchen and out the back door, not wanting to let the cold air in by leaving through the French windows. I looked back at the brightly lit group as I walked through the dark back yard, popping in back home to let John know that I was now on my way up the hill.

I would have preferred walking through the woods up to Highfields but because the sun set so early, I did not wish to stumble along the dark path, even with a flashlight. Instead, I took Glenda's car, relishing my independence and the extra income this job afforded, short-lived as it might be.

The big house was entirely lit up as usual and I drove around the back to park, entering the kitchen filled with the savory scent of pastry baking.

"Oh, Elsie, what are you making?" I asked as I took off my coat.

"Haven't you just come from the tea group? You can't possibly be famished if Annie was up to her usual standards," she answered.

"Annie was and I thought I was stuffed, but whatever is in the oven is making me hungry all over again."

"Shepherd's pie, by request of Mr. Schaeffer. That shouldn't be the name of it since it's not lamb but venison. Hunter's pie, it should be called. He brought the meat with him from the City." She came closer to me to whisper, "The secret is in the spices. I put in rosemary and a touch of juniper berries." She tapped the side of her nose to ensure the secret was safe.

"Where in the world did you learn that?"

"Reverend Lewis inherited the parsonage along with a long shelf of cookbooks, some from the previous century. That's what I would read while something was baking in the oven. It had the strangest language for measurements, like of gill of white wine. And sometimes I couldn't figure out how many pounds of meat was called for when it said, 'take a large roast of beef.' How big was the roast? How big was the animal? It was kind of funny. But it did give me some interesting ideas of the flavors that people liked, such as vinegar in sauces and capers. Can you imagine?"

The notion of putting vinegar in anything but salad dressing was an odd idea for me.

"So, what's the latest?" Elsie said, sitting down across from me at the butcher block table.

"Mrs. Proctor shared her views on one thing and another," I began, and Elsie rolled her eyes, knowing exactly how that conversation must have gone. I lowered my voice. "The women seemed curious about what was going on up here at the house and why so many people had come to Adams in relation to the Schaeffers."

"There were quite a few visitors today, but I'm stuck back here and have no idea what it was all about. I hear the doorbell ring and some loud voices coming from the front of the house, but Mr. Schaeffer does have a big sound to him."

"I know some came to see attorneys in town, the ones down the hall from us in Adams. And one of them was an ex-wife of our employer."

Elsie's eyebrows shot up. "That is interesting. I'd know a great deal more if any of those maids would open their mouths around me, but whenever I appear, they clam up."

"Strange household," I said. "I'm early, but I'll go upstairs and see how Mrs. Schaeffer is doing."

The rooms I walked through were quiet, and as I mounted the stairs, I could again smell the cigar smoke that came from the study at the end of the hall beneath me. One of the maids was walking down the hall toward me with an armful of folded towels, and although she nodded at me, there was no expression on her face. Odd household, indeed.

I knocked on the door and entered Mrs. Schaeffer's bedroom where she sat upright in bed reading a travel magazine.

"Oh, hello," she said brightly.

"That looks interesting," I said. I almost asked if she were planning on going somewhere but bit my tongue.

"It's all about winter sports in Switzerland. I can't imagine traveling halfway around to world to be colder than I am here! I never was the sporty type, anyway. I was a dancer and too aware of protecting my ankles and feet. The notion of strapping long pieces of wood onto my feet and sailing down an icy hill, waiting for an accident to happen!" She shivered. "Still, I think the part of sitting around a fire in casual clothes and furs, sipping whatever it is these folks are drinking, is appealing. And the scenery is gorgeous." She showed me a page of high, snow-covered peaks. "Have you ever been?"

"I'm afraid I've never been out of the country except to Canada. But my husband wants to go on a ski holiday sometime this winter and it might be me who is strapped into those long pieces of wood."

"Oh, dear. Be very careful. In my experience, husbands are of the opinion that whatever they like to do, you'll like to do. That's nonsense, of course. I love to shop but I couldn't get Theo to step in a store with me for the life of him. 'Waste of time,' he'd say. Just as well. I can take my time and charge anything that catches my eye. In keeping with his usual stingy ways, he always barks about the bill but in my case never complains about the outcome." She smiled. "Come sit and tell me what's happening in the great world."

"All sorts of things going on in Germany and Europe. Elections and anarchists acting up. And the United States Congress passed a joint resolution to do away with Prohibition and let the states figure it out. I don't know what that means, exactly."

"Oh, my, it's about time. Anyone who wants to drink manages to do it anyway. What a silly law. I heard from some friends that Detroit and Buffalo have become quite prosperous with a lot of liquor coming across the border by land and by boat. They don't have enough police to stop the traffic. And think of all the nightclubs that have suffered business because of it. Although, come to think of it, there are probably more speakeasies and nightclubs than before. You know, if you forbid someone to do something, it's like a dare to do it."

"Exactly," I said. "Can I get you anything?"

"If you mean a cocktail, no, I'm not allowed." She smiled. "Really, nothing just yet. What's the local gossip?"

"Nothing interesting. The flu is going around and the measles."

She gave me a sharp look. "That hardly interests me. What is all this coming and going in my house?" She drilled her eyes into mine.

"I only got here. Have there been visitors?" I asked innocently.

"We lived quietly in a building in the City with doormen so nobody could bother us. Then Theo thought he was so smart buying an out-of-the-way place for us to live and it turns out someone spilled the beans and now we are flooded with everyone who ever had a grudge against him. And no doorman to fend off the hordes. Well, it's not my affair. Any bad dealings in business he had were not my doing. But I'm sure at least one ex-wife is out to get more alimony from him."

I pretended surprise. "Can she do that?"

"After a judge already made a decision in the case? Probably not. Unless she is pleading some kind of hardship, but even so, who isn't experiencing difficulties in these times?"

I thought that was an odd thing for her to say, as she thumbed through a magazine, living in luxury in a massive house in a beautiful part of the country, someone to look after her needs around the clock.

There was a knock on the door and one of maids came in. "Nurse Taylor, Mr. Schaeffer would like to have a word with you."

"Now?"

"In a few minutes," she said and left.

"It seems you have been able to travel quite a bit," I said, inviting her into a long conversation.

"I met my husband in New York where I was performing but I had several years behind me of traveling around the country and then to England. That was wonderful. Being courted by gentlemen there—very polite and courteous they were, too. An earl even went so far as to propose to me." She laughed. "He was very nice but had horrible teeth and no chin. And terribly boring. His family would never have allowed it and I did the gracious thing by letting him down gently." She sighed. "I suppose he could have gotten his teeth fixed." She giggled. "But 'Mummy' could not be appeased by my presence no matter what I did, I'm sure. I met him in London, and we managed to have fun. But the reality is that those folks mostly live in the country where it's terribly dull. You are expected to ride and hunt, and I don't know what else. It's the men that get to go up to London and have a good time. I don't regret my decision." Still, she smiled at the memory of what might have been.

We heard heavy footsteps coming down the hall in our direction at the same time that a telephone rang in the distance.

"Mr. Schaeffer, phone's for you," one of the maids said from just outside the bedroom door.

There was a grumbled response and the footsteps retreated. A few minutes later, one of the maids reappeared. I couldn't tell if it was the one who had been there previously since they looked remarkably similar.

"Sorry, Miss," she said to me. "Mr. Schaeffer wanted to give you this in person, but he was called away to the telephone." She handed me an envelope. We all looked at it and I wondered if they expected me to open it there and then.

"Your pay, I expect," Mrs. Schaeffer said. "He likes doing everything in cash."

This was my first full day here and he wanted to pay me already? Did that mean he wasn't entirely sure whether I would continue, or was it that he suspected I might quit?

The maid bobbed and left, and I prompted my patient to tell me more about her European travels and adventures. It turned out to be a good topic as she had much to relate to me about places I had heard of and some I didn't know of but was then curious to read about. While educating me, she was entertaining herself.

"Am I tiring you out?" I asked finally.

"Not at all. I've seen so much in my life and remembering it now brings it all back with happy memories."

A knock on the door produced a maid with a tray with Mrs. Schaeffer's dinner. I glanced at my watch and saw it was seven-thirty already.

"I'd better be going," I said, standing up.

"Do stay," Mrs. Schaeffer said.

I looked down at her meager meal and my stomach grumbled. I let her know that I was expected at home and if I stayed any longer, I might snatch the food from her plate.

"Have a lovely evening, my dear. I'll see you tomorrow."

I went down the stairs, the smell of cigar smoke strong as I reached the bottom steps, just adjacent to Mr. Schaeffer's study. What little I had seen of him suggested he only smoked in his study, which was a blessing.

I passed through the dining room where the table was set for one although he was not there, and through the swinging door to the kitchen, still smelling of the shepherd's pie although Elsie was long gone and there was no food in sight. It must have gone down to the servants' dining room in the basement. But what about Mr. Schaeffer's portion? That wasn't my problem to solve.

When I got home, I rushed to John who stood at the stove, looking into a saucepan. I put my arms around him from behind and rested my head on his back.

"What's the matter?"

"Sorry I'm late. I got caught up in Mrs. Schaeffer's recollections. What a fun life she has had and how awful that she'll probably end it here stuck in bed most of the day, not knowing anyone in town, her husband a grumpy man with a list of enemies as long as your arm. I just feel very sorry for her."

Chapter 8

While John and I traded off on making dinner, I was the breakfast cook, up early, perking the coffee, frying the bacon and eggs one day, French toast another and sometimes oatmeal although that always seemed to take so long with all the standing and stirring. He was still upstairs getting dressed the next morning, while I was in my bathrobe, not wanting to soil my uniform that early in the day. That was important since part of my move into my own house meant dealing with the laundry task of maintaining my starched white uniform.

The phone rang and before I could get it, I could hear John's footsteps overhead as he walked to the extension. If he were needed right away, I hoped he would eat some breakfast, at least. His steps were measured as he descended from the second floor, rather than hurried, so perhaps it was not an emergency.

"Who was it?" I asked, half looking over my shoulder from my position at the stove.

"Officer Reed. There's been a death at Highfields."

My shoulders slumped in dismay, and I turned off the gas flame. "Oh, the poor woman."

"No, not Mrs. Schaeffer. Mr. Schaeffer died in his sleep."

I spun around to look at him. I couldn't take it in at first.

"Reed will want to have Gladstone in to help and since he's driving from Pittsfield, I will have time to sit down and have breakfast. But why not come up to the house with me and be of some comfort to his wife?"

I grabbed a piece of toast and went upstairs to get ready, still in a daze. Sure, he was overweight, smoked, drank and seemingly ate like a horse, but what a shock. I wondered how she was taking it and if she was ready to deal with all the details with her own health being precarious. Although I still didn't know if she was fully aware of her situation. So much to be done after a person dies and his affairs seemed more complicated than most. My thoughts went to his ex-wife who had wanted an increase in her alimony. That wasn't going to happen now; in fact, it was the end of her allowance. The consolation for her was that she was now able to marry her boyfriend, but what would they live on? I put their problems out of my mind and hurried to put on my stockings.

We parked in front at Highfields and rang the bell that was answered by one of the look-alike maids who had her head down, her face nearly concealed by the headache band, the thick hair and the glasses. She didn't say a word but ushered us in. She looked at the staircase and then back at us and it made me wonder if she were mute or just shocked into lack of speech.

"We know the way up," John said to her, and we climbed the stairs. I knew where Mrs. Schaeffer's room was, of course, but didn't know which was Mr. Schaeffer's bedroom. The question was answered when I saw an open door at the opposite end of the hall with Officer Reed standing outside.

"Thanks for coming," he said.

"Who called this in?" John asked.

"One of the maids noticed that a pane in the kitchen door's window had been broken, just where someone would want to reach in to access the lock inside. There was mud tracked in but nothing much in the way of clear footprints. The maid," here he stopped and took out his small notebook for reference, "Bess is her name, went up to tell Mr. Schaeffer and found him lifeless in his bed. She said she was terrified that someone had broken in and was still in the house but got up the nerve to ring the operator and put a call into us."

I looked around me, thinking that in a house this large, someone could easily find a hiding place and stay there until things became quieter. I certainly hoped he wasn't still lurking about. But if that person had not come in to burgle the house but to harm Mr. Schaeffer, he would have wanted to leave immediately. Although we didn't yet know the nature of the death.

"Let's take a look," John said and went in to examine the supine body, first making sure that he was indeed deceased. Mr. Schaeffer was lined up neatly, the covers folded back as if the bed had been made around him with his hands folded one over the other. John palpated the arms and legs and said, "He's been dead quite some time."

"I heard him last night just before I left, close to seven-thirty," I said.

"Hmph. Seems longer than that."

"He was right outside his wife's bedroom when he was called to the telephone. I heard him grumble something to the maid before he walked away."

"We can get a more precise time after we take the body away."

Mr. Schaeffer looked peaceful without the sneer on his face although I wouldn't have said he was attractive.

"I wonder if he had any heart problems?" John muttered to himself before sniffing at the man's face, then pulling the covers down and seeing the perfectly smoothed-out fabric of the striped pajama shirt.

He took one of the stiff hands and looked at both sides, then pushed the sleeve as far as it would go to the elbow and replaced it. "Hmph." He said again. "Well, we'd better call the funeral home in Adams."

"Would you like to look in on Mrs. Schaeffer?" Officer Reed asked.

"Yes, we'd better. How is she taking it?"

"She seemed more surprised than shocked. And when she heard the bit about someone having broken in, she became agitated. You can't blame her for being afraid in the big house with the maids sleeping on the third floor and she all alone down here."

"She's not quite alone. I understand one of the maids sleeps in the next room. But still…." I thought I would be anxious in her shoes.

"I'll go downstairs to look at the entry place again," Officer Reed said.

Mrs. Schaeffer was in her hospital bed, looking toward the windows when we came in her room. She was her usual pale self but composed as she nodded in greeting.

"I'm so sorry," John said, taking her hand. I was near tears, not primarily for her husband's demise, but for her sense of loss and the lack of support she faced with her debilitating illness.

"Can I get you anything?" I asked her.

"No, I don't think so. Is what they told me true? That someone broke into the house?"

"From what Officer Reed told us, it appears that way."

"Was anything taken or disturbed?"

John shrugged. "I don't know if anyone has thought to take inventory. Did your husband have a safe or money in the house?"

"Cash, of course. And he did have a safe. But are the two events connected? Do you think the person may have gone into Theo's bedroom and he was so frightened that he…."

"Had a heart attack? Perhaps. Did he have a history of heart problems?"

"His doctor in New York was trying to get him to give up smoking, to no avail. But I suppose that is sound advice no matter what condition your health is in. Did anybody hear someone creeping about?"

"I couldn't say. I don't know if Officer Reed has questioned any of the staff yet."

"Have you had breakfast?" I asked her, going into nurse mode.

"No."

"I'll see if Elsie is here and rustle up some tea at least."

John stayed with his patient, and I went down to the kitchen, not seeing any of the maids anywhere. Sam had just dropped Elsie off and she was standing in the room with her coat still on, looking at Officer Reed.

"What's happened here?" she asked, her boots crunching on the shards of glass as she walked from the door.

"It looks like someone may have broken in. And Mr. Schaeffer has died."

Her eyes were wide. "How did he die?"

"We're not sure yet," Reed said. "But those two events happened sometime in the night."

"Did they take anything?" she asked.

"We don't know yet. We don't know what there is to be stolen."

Still in her overcoat, she pushed the swinging door to the dining room open and walked to the closets that lined one wall. They were not locked and when she opened them, we could see the sparkling glassware and silver, row upon row.

"Well, they didn't come for that, I guess." She closed the door and opened the next closet with the same results.

"Elsie, it seems because of all the turmoil, none of the maids has brought tea up to Mrs. Schaeffer yet. I don't know what she has for breakfast, but she ought to have something to eat with the shock and all."

"Of course," she replied, finally taking her coat off and marching back into the kitchen to put the kettle on to boil. "Tom, would you like some coffee?"

"That would be just the thing," he said. "Been out here for some time this morning."

She filled the percolator with water and then the carefully put the coffee grounds into the filter basket. "Strong?" she asked.

"Ah, yes."

While that was set on the stove to boil, she said, "I made scones yesterday. They're not fresh, but I'll warm them in the oven."

I had already had a bit of breakfast, but this was making me hungry for more. I decided to wander in the house until the kettle boiled since I hadn't been in all the downstairs rooms for some time. The sitting room was spectacular with views of Mount Greylock now with a ring of mist of around it; I could sit here all day admiring the view. If you got close to the windows, you could see who was coming up the drive, which at that moment I deduced was Inspector Gladstone in his familiar black car.

I could have hustled out of the sitting room and back into the kitchen before he got to the doorbell, but I decided to hold my ground. After all, he might decide to check out Mr. Schaeffer's bedroom first. As luck would have it, the maid who answered the door ushered him into the sitting room where he stopped in his tracks upon seeing me.

"Good morning," I said solemnly.

"It may be a good morning for some," he grumbled, removing his hat.

The maid who stood next to him reached for the hat and received the overcoat he piled into her arms. She scurried away before he realized he meant to ask her where the late Mr. Schaeffer was and so he scowled at me instead.

"I suppose you know where the body is," he said.

"Yes, if you'll follow me," I said. As I passed by him, I smelled aromatic pipe smoke emanating from his clothes. That was a surprise. It made me think he often sat in his office puffing on a meerschaum and puzzling out the trail of clues in some case. But no, I must have been thinking of Sherlock Holmes.

"Where is everyone?" he asked as we climbed the stairs.

"Mrs. Schaeffer is in her room at the end of the hall with Doctor Taylor. The cook is in the kitchen with Officer Reed."

"No surprise there. And the servants?"

"I have no idea. Aside from the one you just saw, they seemed to have vanished."

"They haven't fled the scene, have they?"

"I just meant that they have made themselves scarce, that's all. They may be in their rooms under the eaves or toiling in the basement." I don't know why I was speaking that way, but it fed into his already formed impression of me as someone above herself.

"That is Mr. Schaeffer's room." I gestured.

"Who else has been in there?"

"Doctor Taylor and I arrived a short time ago and we went in with Officer Reed. You'd have to ask him about who else had access. If you'll excuse me," I said, turning away.

"Where are you going?"

"To the kitchen to get some tea for Mrs. Schaeffer. By the way, Elsie the cook is making coffee to go with some scones, if you need warming up."

He gave me a look that suggested I had made a play on words, but I ignored it and returned downstairs.

The teapot had been filled, a tray readied and a scone with currants sat in the middle of a plate. Officer Reed was relaxed and content with his breakfast—possibly his second of the day—when I broke his reverie to let him know that Gladstone was upstairs. He practically jumped off the stool and hurried away, wiping the crumbs off his face with the back of his hand.

"Where are the maids?" I asked, seeing that the task of delivering should have been theirs. Not that I minded doing it, I was just apprehensive about walking up the staircase with a tray of food, something I had rarely done before. It reminded me of the first time I had bought a hot lunch in elementary school and had to navigate to a bench, certain I would trip or allow the contents to slide off onto another student.

I reached my destination without mishap and found John and Mrs. Schaeffer in a calm conversation with her earlier anxiety subdued. What a wonderful bedside manner he had to be able to do that.

"Here we are," I said, placing the tray on the wide bedside table before realizing it should go onto her lap. I would be a disaster as a maid, I realized. "Inspector Gladstone is here," I said, and John got up.

"I should probably accompany him," he said, leaving the room.

"This is such an extraordinary event," she said. "Since my illness, we haven't shared a bedroom, so though he would come to say goodnight, I wouldn't see him until morning. And sometimes, he had business or an early telephone call and I wouldn't see him until later in the day. I keep thinking he is just down the hall, still asleep. Or down in his study smoking a cigar and talking on the phone."

I didn't say anything.

"And we both thought I would go first," she said, pouring some tea for herself. "Do you think I ought to see him one last time? To let the reality sink in? Or am I supposed to say one last goodbye?"

How could I respond to her questions? I couldn't, so I got up and tidied around the bed while she sipped her tea. Finally, I felt I was not providing appropriate comfort and said, "This must be so difficult for you. I'm sorry that I don't know what to say or do at this moment."

That came out all wrong and it made it seem as if I expected her to guide me in what to do, which was not my intent.

"There, there," she said, patting my hand. I should have been patting hers.

"The inspector was asking where the maids were, and I have only seen the one who answered the door."

"How odd. I told Theo that we should have hired a housekeeper to manage the staff, but he was either too preoccupied with the move or his business to do that. I certainly can't perform that function from a hospital bed." She looked over at me and I hope she didn't think I would take on that responsibility.

"I'm sure the agency you contacted to hire those young women in the first place could assist."

"That's a good idea. Or I could just let them run amuck doing what they have been doing all along. And what that is, I have no idea, being stuck in this room all day." She nibbled on the scone, and I excused myself to see what John was doing.

Officer Reed, Inspector Gladstone and John were standing outside Mr. Schaeffer's room talking in low tones when the doorbell rang. I look over the banister and saw one of the maids walk quickly to the front door, then gasp slightly as she saw two men with a stretcher standing outside. She let them in and preceded them down the hall and up the stairs, gesturing toward the bedroom before going toward the door to the backstairs and out of sight.

"Here they are," said Officer Reed unnecessarily as he led them into the bedroom.

"I'm not the one to do an autopsy if that is required. That might be Doctor Schell in Pittsfield. But I'll follow them back to the funeral home and make a more thorough examination than I did previously."

"Why is that?" Gladstone asked.

"Rigor mortis has set in, and I didn't want to disturb the body that much. I also wanted to alert the mortuary staff to carefully note when rigor dissipates, which will give a better idea of time of death." He looked over at me. "Aggie, how about if I drop you off back home? If you can open the Adams office by yourself, I don't think I'll be too much longer."

I agreed and suggested that one of the maids or Elsie should look in on Mrs. Schaeffer until I got back again for my evening shift.

"Wait," Gladstone said. "Were you here last evening?"

"Yes, from about four forty-five until seven thirty."

"Well then, I need to speak with you."

"That's fine, but we have a medical practice with patients coming in that we need to attend to. If you stop by the office in the Professional Building in Adams, second floor, I'll be there until noon. Then we move back to the West Adams location for the afternoon."

He scratched his wiry hair and look perplexed. "That's a busy schedule."

"Yes, it is. I'll just get my coat," I said. I went down to the kitchen and let Elsie know that I was leaving and suggested that she get one or more of the maids to look in on Mrs. Schaeffer as they had been scarce since I arrived.

"Those girls," she muttered. "I'll have to climb all the way to the third floor to find them, if that's where they are, sitting in their rooms, reading movie magazines, no doubt." She wasn't too much older than I, but her pronouncements sometimes made her seem as if she were older.

Why shouldn't they sit in their rooms waiting to be called to perform some function? In previous visits, they were bustling all over the house, carrying things from room to room. That made me stop and think a moment. I had witnessed them answering the door, carrying a tray upstairs to Mrs. Schaeffer, but aside from that I never saw them actually do anything else. They didn't dust or vacuum, they didn't wash the dishes or prepare the food. Their only function seemed to be carrying piles of towels or linens and making themselves as innocuous as possible.

Chapter 9

I was feeling overwhelmed by the events of the day and aware that I would probably be swamped with rescheduling the appointments that had been made if John were gone for some time. Although I managed to get to the Adams office before nine o'clock, there was somebody already waiting to get in and looking peeved that the door was locked. It was a handsome young man who looked somewhat familiar, but by this time I had begun to recognize many of the local people by sight.

"Good morning," I said. "Are you waiting to see the doctor?" I asked as I opened the door and turned on the light.

"Yes, I seem to have broken my finger." He held up his right hand to show me the crooked pinky.

"That must have hurt," I said, taking off my overcoat and inviting him to do the same as there was a coat rack adjacent to the reception chairs.

"The doctor isn't here yet, but if you can fill out this health form, he should be here within the hour."

His shoulders slumped but he took the clipboard with the sheet of paper I offered him and hesitated before filling it out. Something about the tilt of his head made me think I had seen him before, but not here in town. I sat down behind my desk to look over the appointments and saw that they were skewed toward later in the morning so perhaps rescheduling wouldn't be necessary. I went into John's office, closed the door and looked up the telephone number of the funeral home. I asked if John was still there and learned that he had just left. Good, this poor young man wouldn't have to wait long.

I busied myself with filing and couldn't help feeling his eyes on me and I looked up.

"Are you from around here?" I asked.

"No, from out of town. I'm here on family business." He put his head back down and scratched on the paper with his fountain pen. He stood and delivered the clipboard to me.

"Doctor Taylor will be here shortly."

He cocked his head to one side briefly and I looked down at his health form. His name was Otis Schaeffer. I looked up abruptly. "Are you here to see Mr. Schaeffer of Highfields?" I asked.

"Yes, he's my father. My estranged father, I should say."

Everything became clear as I looked down at the name Otis. The last person I had encountered with that first name was a certain Otis Warren, who claimed to be the long-lost son of the deceased Mr. Browne whose widow, Hextilda, lived in Boston. We had met this young man and his mother, who had once been a secretary to the family, at the Brownes' home in Beacon Hill the previous February. Although his claim could have been genuine, I never found out if it had been pursued or resolved. Now, here was the same young man purporting to be the son of Mr. Schaeffer. Was this a scam he and his mother—if indeed she was his mother—perpetrated on wealthy families?

If I appeared shocked, it was real, but not for the reason he may have imagined. He couldn't possibly know that his purported father was already dead, and I wasn't going to be the one to tell him. But why had he chosen this time to come to the Berkshires to assert his relationship, if that was his intent? I couldn't understand why the Schaeffers' move to our part of the world had engendered so much interest from other places. And I couldn't help but notice that his expensive fountain pen had the initials O.W. on the gold band. This young man needed to be more careful about details!

He managed a self-effacing smile, which I took to be as authentic as his heritage claims, and got back to my paperwork. Some minutes later, John came in and I pointedly said, "Good morning, Doctor Taylor."

Now the connection clicked with Otis, recognizing the doctor more readily than identifying me, who had been in an evening dress the last time we had encountered each other, not in a white uniform. His eyes darted from John to me, and I thought he was about to dash out the door, but he pulled himself together and bluffed it out.

"How nice to meet you, Doctor Taylor. I would shake your hand except I seem to have broken a finger and it would be a painful experience for me." He smiled broadly and John took off his overcoat and said he would be ready in a few minutes, repairing to his office to put on his white coat before exiting again to the reception area. He led the patient into the exam room, and I decided to let the situation run its course without my giving away the game just yet.

I could hear them in conversation and drawers opening as John probably took out a cushioned metal splint. After one yelp as he set the digit straight, it was quiet as he likely wrapped up the finger. John opened the door and said, "Take some aspirin for the pain, if you need it. It will heal in a surprisingly short time. And watch how you shut the door in the future!"

All smiles, Otis took up his overcoat and left the office.

After he was gone, I asked, "You didn't recognize him?"

"It's terrible to admit, but the more patients I see, the more I think I've seen them before."

"He wasn't a patient."

John looked at me quizzically.

"Think back to the Valentine Ball in Boston and the cocktail hour at your friend Fred Browne's home, where his mother Hextilda had unexpected visitors."

His eyes widened. "But?"

"Yes, at that time, this young man was the unacknowledged son of good old Mr. Browne, conveniently deceased so as not to admit or deny his dalliance with the secretary, Vera Hamilton. That didn't get any traction. Why not seek out another wealthy man to call Daddy?" I asked. "He now claims he is Theodore Schaeffer's son."

"But only a few people know that Mr. Schaeffer has died. If he expected to confront him, thinking he was still alive, that would be a difficult proposition."

"What if he knew he was already dead? What if he had some role in it?"

John sat down heavily in the chair next to my desk. "This is getting complicated. I didn't have an opportunity to tell you when I first came in, with the young man standing there, but my exam at the funeral home was more extensive than what I was able to conduct at the house. Once his pajama shirt was removed, I could see extensive bruising on his upper and lower arms. The reason I wanted a closer look was that he seemed posed in that bed with the covers neatly arranged with his hands folded over."

"Yes, who sleeps like that?" I waited for more.

"It looks like he had been held down. That led me to examine his face and mouth more closely and it seems he had a few strands of cloth between his teeth. As if someone had suffocated him with a pillow and he resisted before succumbing."

"If that's true, it couldn't have been his wife, she's too weak. And it couldn't have been young Otis because he wasn't aware of the death."

"Or pretended not to know of it," John said.

We were both startled when the door opened suddenly, but it was only Inspector Gladstone, and I sighed with relief.

"I'm glad I am welcome at last. Who were you expecting?" he asked with a bit of a smile.

"I know you're here to interview Aggie, but I just came from the funeral home after a more thorough examination of Mr. Schaeffer's body," John said. He then relayed to the inspector his observations and I told him about Otis turning up seeking yet another father.

He sank slowly onto one of the reception chairs and shook his head. "This thing is getting to be stranger by the minute. But, Nurse Taylor," he began, a bit unsure of what to call me. "I'm here to have an interview with you, if you have the time."

"Certainly. John, may we use your office?"

He agreed and the inspector removed his coat and slung it over his arm. This was the first time he was overtly courteous to me, and I wondered if it was because I was married. The ever-present small notebook was pulled out and he began. "How long have you known the Schaeffers?"

"Only since they moved into Highfields."

"Yet they knew to hire you as a private nurse?"

"Well, I think I am the only nurse in West Adams, so that wasn't too hard a decision. But I suspect that Cash Ridley, who knew Mr. Schaeffer in New York, may have had a hand in it, too."

"What are your work hours?"

"They asked me to come between five and seven o'clock at night. I don't know why they chose those hours, perhaps that's when Mr.

Schaeffer had dinner, or the staff was eating, and his wife would be alone. She took her meals on a tray in her bedroom."

"How did they come to hire Elsie to cook for them? I thought she worked for Reverend Lewis."

"She did but left after she got married this year. I don't know who recommended her, but she said that with things being slow at the farm in the winter, she might as well earn some money. And I gather they pay her well." I paused to think. "Perhaps Cash Ridley had a hand in that, too. I don't know."

"Tell me what happened last night."

"I arrived before five o'clock and chatted with Elsie for a bit then went upstairs to see if Mrs. Schaeffer needed anything. I sat with her, and she was very talkative, telling me about places where she had traveled and interesting characters she had met. One of the maids came to the door and said that Mr. Schaeffer wanted to talk to me. Not right then, I guess, because she left, and we continued our conversation. Sometime later, we could hear Mr. Schaeffer coming down the hall at about the same time as the telephone rang. I heard one of the maids tell him the call was for him and he muttered something and walked away to take the call. The maid came to the bedroom and handed me an envelope that he had wanted to give me. I assumed it was my pay and I thought it a bit crass to open it right then, so I tucked it into my pocket."

"And then?"

"We kept talking and I realized that it was getting late. In fact it was about a half hour longer than I intended to be there. So, I said goodbye and left."

"Did you see Mr. Schaeffer as you went out?"

"No, I don't know where he was. I could certainly smell the cigar smoke as I went down the stairs, and I assumed he was in his study."

"Did you hear him talking on the telephone?"

"No, I didn't hear anyone. I don't know where the maids go to have their meals, but the dining room table was set for one, so I suppose he hadn't had his dinner yet."

"Where was Elsie?"

"She left much earlier, I think. She cooks the meals, but it must be one of the maids who does the actual serving because Elsie took the job under the condition that she wouldn't be there all day long."

"Did you go out the front door or the kitchen door?"

"The kitchen door."

"And was the window broken at that time?"

"Certainly not. I would have noticed or stepped on the broken glass."

"Was the door locked?"

"I don't know. There isn't a housekeeper as such, so I don't know who makes sure that things are battened down at the end of the day. All I know is I could get out."

"That's bad management in a house that large and isolated. Well, the door must have got locked at some point, otherwise why would someone need to break the glass to get in?" he asked.

"True," I agreed.

"What do you make of the servants?"

"What do you mean?"

"They're a strange bunch." He looked up from under his shaggy eyebrows to see my reaction.

"How so?" I was keeping my observations to myself for the time being.

"From what I've heard and observed, some look surprisingly alike. Same hair, same clothes, same glasses."

"The uniform can't be helped, I suppose. And the hairstyle is what many young women wear these days. The glasses, well, necessary, wouldn't you say?"

"Here's what's really odd. I spoke to one of them and she said she wouldn't talk to me alone in a room. She said they would want another female present."

So, that was why he was being so nice. He wanted me to spend my idle hours as a proctor during the interviews.

"Why hasn't Mrs. Schaeffer agreed to do it?"

"She's much too ill. I didn't want to ask her."

"What about Elsie?"

"She flat out refused."

I had to laugh at her strength of character; she was not cowed by Inspector Gladstone. Neither was I, but if he was in a pickle, I supposed I could help him out. It wouldn't hurt to be in his good books for a change.

"All right, but I'll have to see if Doctor Taylor can afford to let me go for a few hours."

He gave a look. "You don't really think he'll say no, do you?"

"No," I admitted.

"And do you call him Doctor Taylor all the time?" he added with a bit of a leer.

I stood up. "Let me know anytime you're thinking of needing me to be a chaperone."

Chapter 10

Since Inspector Gladstone was always in a hurry, he telephoned back after lunch to say he had arranged for a four o'clock time at Highfields. It wouldn't cut into John's schedule too much and I could segue seamlessly into my early evening appointment with Mrs. Schaeffer.

He and Officer Reed were waiting outside the front door of the house as I drove up and I stopped to let him know that, in my capacity as an employee, I went in through the kitchen door. They continued to stand on the front steps.

"I'll meet you inside," I said. The silly men didn't know that Elsie had likely baked some treats that would go well with the cup of coffee she would offer me. She was surprised to see me so early and I explained my errand.

"That is the strangest thing I ever heard," she said. "And it's why I said no to his request. I don't want to know everybody's secrets, especially those of people who I work with every day. And they don't need to know mine." She gave a small laugh.

"Elsie, now you've got me curious. What are you hiding?"

"You'll find out soon enough," she said, and I tried not to be so obvious as to stare at her stomach, hidden behind the large white apron, although that was likely the secret.

I walked through the house to the front door where Gladstone and Officer Reed stood, with one of the maids looking terrified nearby.

"Hello, I'm sorry, I don't know your name," I said to her.

She cleared her throat and said, "Nan. Nan Johnson."

I held out my hand. "I'm Aggie Taylor."

"I know."

"Inspector Gladstone asked me to sit in on the interviews. I hope that is all right with you?" He shot me a look indicating he didn't think permission was necessary, but I intended to be polite and non-threatening.

"Which room can we use?" he asked her.

She looked at me as if it were my decision. Well, then. "How about the morning room? It's cozy in there." I led the way and she timidly followed.

We sat at the small round table while Gladstone removed his overcoat, undid the button of his jacket and fussed about looking for his notebook and something to write with. He settled on a pencil fished out of his jacket pocket along with a ball of lint that he scowled at before flicking it onto the carpet.

I had been looking at Nan more closely and focused on her brown hair that had a strange, coarse consistency, and seemed to not move naturally so she pulled one side forward to partly conceal her face. Then the poor girl twisted her hands in her lap and sat on the edge of the chair awaiting the worst, it seemed.

"Now then, where were you last evening around eight o'clock?"

I didn't know why he chose that time. Presumably because I had heard Mr. Schaeffer sometime before I left at seven-thirty.

"Here," she said in a barely audible voice.

He huffed in annoyance. "In this room? Or where in the house?"

"I'm not sure. About that time, I would be clearing the table downstairs after our supper."

"I'm not interested in what you *would* be doing. What *were* you doing?"

"Clearing the table. I don't know, I don't own a watch."

I glared at the inspector as I thought she was about to burst into tears. He nodded and softened his tone.

"How did you come to have this job in the first place?"

"Through the agency."

"Which agency?"

"An employment agency in New York. It's called Domestics, I think. I signed up after my other job went away."

"What was that?"

"I worked for another household in Manhattan, but they came on hard times and said they couldn't afford to keep me on any longer."

"Before we're done, I'd like you to give me the name and address of that former employer."

She nodded.

"Do you have any family?"

"Here?" she asked.

"No, I meant any family in New York or somewhere else."

"No, I was raised in an orphanage."

He cleared his throat and searched for something to ask her. I was getting annoyed at what a pointless task it was to have me present but said nothing.

"Did you hear or see anything unusual last night?"

"No."

"Did Mr. Schaeffer come to dinner?"

She stared at him.

"I don't know. It's not my job to serve him at supper."

"Is there anything else you'd like to tell me?"

She was leaning forward, about to get up and then said, "Don't trust what some of the other girls tell you. Some of them are liars." With that, she got out of the chair and walked quickly out of the room.

Gladstone looked at me and shook his head. "Can you bring in the next girl?" he said to me. That wasn't what I had agreed to, and I wasn't his employee. I turned to Officer Reed, who got up swiftly.

"Where are they? In the kitchen?"

"I don't know."

He disappeared and was gone about five minutes before returning with another maid, who looked much like Nan in height, weight and the tendency to hide behind her hair when being questioned.

I introduced myself to her and she said her name was Bess Williams. She looked as uncomfortable as Nan had and stared at the hands in her lap.

Gladstone went through the same questions with her, and she said she had neither seen nor heard anything unusual the previous night. She hadn't served Mr. Schaeffer dinner, either, and was busy putting away some linens.

"Did you answer the phone last night?" he asked.

"No, that's not my job. June does that."

She named the same agency that Nan had cited as the source of her employment at Highfields and said she had worked in a restaurant previously. Her family lived in New Jersey, and she had shared an apartment with several other girls from work.

"How did you happen to hear of this job?"

"I wasn't making very much from the other place, and someone told me about an agency that employed domestic servants and I thought I would apply. I was surprised that they contacted me and offered me transportation up here, salary and room and board."

"How do you like working here?" he asked. That seemed an out-of-character question for Gladstone, but he wasn't getting much out of this young woman.

"It's fine."

"So, what was your task last night?"

"I wash up the dishes after the meal."

"The servants' dishes or Mr. Schaeffer's?"

"Our own dishes. I think the cook must clean up after Mr. Schaeffer."

That couldn't be right. Did she think he left his dirty plates out on the table until the morning for Elsie to wash up? I couldn't imagine him bringing his own things into the kitchen and putting them in the sink like a farmer.

"Did he have dinner last night?"

She shrugged.

"Did you hear or see anything unusual?"

"Like the kitchen window being broken and someone creeping about?"

Gladstone's eyes glittered. "Yes, anything like that?"

"No."

Then he glared at her.

"We sleep on the third floor. How could we possibly hear something far away on the first floor in the kitchen? And nobody would break into a house like this to steal something and think there was anything worth taking from the maids' rooms." She snorted at the idea.

"I think that's enough for now," Gladstone said.

She dismissed his comment by blinking her eyes before getting up. As she walked toward the door, she readjusted the back bow of her apron, and I noticed that the seam of her right stocking was not straight. Had she and I been alone, I might have alerted her, but I didn't want to embarrass her with a man in the room. After all, they had requested someone else be present during the interviews, but if it were because of being shy, Bess seemed like she could hold her own in a bar brawl.

June was the next maid in, and it was ridiculous how much she resembled the other two. She sat woodenly in the chair and kept her eyes focused on some spot on the tabletop. I introduced myself and she responded in kind without making eye contact.

"Now, June, can you tell me about the events of last night?"

"What about them?"

"For instance, tell me the mood Mr. Schaeffer was in. Happy, concerned, his usual self?"

"I never saw him last night. I was busy polishing silver in the basement. They have a lot of silver in this house."

"Didn't you answer the phone for him last night?"

"No, I don't answer the phones. That's Jane's job."

Gladstone looked at me and I thought perhaps we had misheard Nan's timid voice saying it was June. The names were similar enough.

"Did you hear the phone ring?"

"Sure, you can hear it ring even in the basement. But we don't pick up the extension down there."

"Okay, then. So, you didn't see Mr. Schaeffer last night?"

"No."

"Did you hear him?"

"I heard someone walking around above in his study. He is a big man, and they were heavy footsteps. When I went up the backstairs later, I could smell the cigar smoke. It gets all over the house."

"I don't suppose you smoke cigars?" Gladstone said by way of being amusing.

She glanced over the rims of her glasses at him briefly but said nothing.

"Did you hear or see anything unusual last night?"

"No. All was quiet as usual. And we're very quiet up in the attic. Mr. Schaeffer told us he wouldn't tolerate any noise from staff."

Gladstone seemed to have run out of questions, and she was dismissed.

"He sounds like a most unpleasant person. But unpleasant enough to suffocate?" Gladstone asked.

"Not by one of those girls. You do know there are a slew of people recently come to town who had axes to grind with Mr. Schaeffer," I said.

"I heard about the ex-wife who wanted more alimony," he said.

"Except killing him would be the end of whatever allowance she was already getting."

"Maybe her fiancé, if that's what they call the man she is shacking up with, got fed up with the situation and lost his temper, came up here, broke in and did the deed."

"He would have had to know the layout of the house, first, and the Schaeffers only just bought this place. He would also have had to be assured that no one would see him breaking and entering, much less trying to find the right bedroom."

"Of course, I know that," Gladstone said.

"You know, John never heard back from the funeral home about the rigor mortis issue, about when it dissipated."

"You mean in order to determine the exact time of death?"

"Yes."

"Good point, I'll follow up on that tomorrow."

"Are we going to continue with these interviews now?" I asked. I thought they were rather pointless.

"Yes, we'd better."

"I'll go get the next girl," I said, eager to stretch my legs. But she was seated in a chair in the hallway waiting to be called and stood up quickly. I introduced myself and led Ann into the room. She nodded at Inspector Gladstone and sat down.

"Terrible business, isn't it?" he began.

She nodded.

"Have you worked for the Schaeffers long?"

"No, I answered an ad in the newspaper looking for domestic help. My mother has a boarding house in Brooklyn, so I know all about cleaning, cooking and so forth. I was desperate to get out and earn my own money, so I applied for the job."

"Was it an agency that did the hiring?"

"No, it was a man who said he worked for the family."

"His name?"

"I can't really remember. He explained that the house wasn't in the City but out in the country. He mentioned the pay and that there was room and board, and I got nervous. Suppose he was a one of those white slavers?"

I hadn't thought of that. These poor girls with little or no family could be easily lured away with such promises and never heard from again.

"Why did you agree?"

"I think he saw I was afraid. But then he introduced me to one of the other girls, Beth, who was sitting in the next room and said she had already signed on. So, I said yes."

It still could have been a dodgy scheme if Beth already worked for the man who had no name, but it turned out to be all right. With the exception that her future employer would soon be dead.

"What were your tasks last night?"

"I was setting the table."

"In the basement?" Gladstone asked, drilling his eyes into her.

"No, up in the dining room where Mr. Schaeffer eats alone. He likes things just so."

"Did you serve him dinner?"

"No, that's not my job. Nan's supposed to do it."

I didn't know if Gladstone was confused, but I couldn't seem to keep the stories straight of who did what and where anyone was. I knew Elsie would have been in the kitchen earlier in the day, but she left at five o'clock and wouldn't know who was where, either.

"Did he eat his dinner?"

"I suppose so," she said.

"Who clears the table after he eats or waits on him?"

"Maybe Bess, I'm not sure."

Nobody seemed to know what anybody else's job was or what anyone was doing. What a mess.

"And I don't suppose you heard anyone breaking in or coming up the stairs?" he asked, not expecting a straight answer.

"Of course not! I would have said something or screamed. Everything was as quiet as usual."

Gladstone looked down at his notes and flipped a few pages and seemed about to ask another question but shook his head as if to clear it instead. "You can go," he concluded.

The last maid was Beth, once again, an exact replica of one of the other girls we had already seen. She pushed her glasses back in position and sat down heavily in the chair.

"Tell me about last night."

"I was doing my usual work and Mr. Schaeffer approached me and told me to take an envelope upstairs."

"Where was he?"

"He stepped out of his study, and I was tidying up in the hallway."

"How did he look?"

"Fine."

"Where were you supposed to take the envelope?"

"I was to give it to Nurse Taylor here, which I did. Remember?" This last remark was directed at me.

"Yes," I said a bit haltingly. I had assumed the girl who delivered the envelope was the same one who told Mr. Schaeffer that the phone call was for him. I don't know why except that I hadn't been in the household long enough to tell them apart.

"What was in the envelope?" Gladstone asked.

"My pay for the time I had already been there."

He directed the next question to the maid. "Is there something you're not telling me?"

She looked down and said softly, "I saw him make a pass at the nurse here."

He looked at me and I could feel the suspicion rising in his face.

"Thank you, Beth, that's all for now."

I watched her leave and noticed the crooked seam on her right stocking but before I could ask her to come back, Gladstone had turned swiftly in my direction.

"He paid you so soon? Before the end of one night's work? The man who everyone said was a tightwad, a miser? That sounds suspicious to me."

"I did think it was strange, but…."

"And maybe he decided to buy your silence with some cash? And perhaps you were so insulted by his presumption that after you left Mrs. Schaeffer, you went to his room where he was asleep and suffocated him."

I stood up, furious. "What an absurd notion! I heard him in the hallway shortly before I left. How could he have been in bed asleep minutes later?"

"Maybe you were mistaken about the time?"

"Mrs. Schaeffer knows when I left, and John knows when I got home. Besides, he was a big man—I couldn't possibly have overcome his strength."

He glared at me, not quite believing my story.

"You haven't been paying any attention to what's going on here," I said. "Look at your notes. Nothing makes sense. Each girl claims someone else must have been doing something and then the next girl contradicts them. Don't you think it's odd that they all look so similar? Didn't you notice that their names are confusing enough?

Jane, June, Bess, Beth, Ann and Nan. All they had to do was mumble and you've mistaken one for the other."

He twisted his mouth to one side, about to concede that his accusation of me was ridiculous and that strange things were indeed going on.

"You didn't even notice that Beth, who was just in here, was actually Bess with the same crooked seam in her stocking. Is there a Beth? Are there six maids or only five? Or four? You'd better call all of them together and see what's going on." I looked at my watch. "I'm going to be late for my shift with Mrs. Schaeffer." I walked toward the door. "You're welcome," I said over my shoulder.

Chapter 11

I detoured to the kitchen first to see if there was a pot of tea to be taken upstairs and to grab a quick cup of coffee to keep me going for the next two hours. The tea had already left the kitchen, Elsie was busy at the stove and the percolator had been put away.

"Have a good evening," I said to her back as I went through the swinging door into the dining room. I stopped and looked at the polished table, which in previous visits had a place setting waiting for the lone diner. I wondered if Mr. Schaeffer had eaten dinner but since the cause of death had been determined to be suffocation, an autopsy hadn't been done which might have revealed it he had eaten a meal. Why did that nag at me so much? I realized because none of the maids could confirm they had seen him sitting down to eat, nor had any of them indicated clearing the table of soiled dishes. And if the dishes hadn't been used, wouldn't someone have wondered where Mr. Schaeffer was? So, who un-set the table?

Could one of the maids be in league with the disgruntled investor or the penurious ex-wife? There was another ex-wife who hadn't shown up yet to my knowledge. Where did she fit in? And Otis, the perennial fatherless man, who was better off now that his alleged 'real' father was gone and unable to refute his claim. Whatever that might be.

As I climbed the stairs, deep in thought, a man exited Mrs. Schaeffer's room. The same man I had first seen when we met. He stopped as I reached the top step.

"You must be Aggie Taylor."

"Yes," I said.

"Nice to meet you," he said holding out his hand. "Mrs. Schaeffer thinks very highly of you."

I'm sure I blushed as I shook his warm hand. In the other hand was a briefcase and he glanced down at it. "Robert Sullivan," he introduced himself, before going down the stairs.

Mrs. Schaeffer was propped up in bed, looking out toward the big windows although it was already dark outside. She heard my approach and smiled.

"I thought you might have forgotten," she said.

"No, just busy downstairs and lost track of time."

"Time. So much to do and so little time. I've just revised my will. Again. Now that Theodore is gone, I might be able to do some good in the world with his money."

I fussed around the night table, and she asked me to sit down.

"What would you do with a large windfall?" she asked.

I laughed. "Since that's not likely to happen to me, I've never given it much thought."

"Buy a car? Get a house?"

"I have those things already," I said.

"And so have I. I thought perhaps I might raise someone out of poverty. Someone who may have suffered needlessly and whose life was affected by the actions of others."

"Do you have some charity in mind? Or were you thinking of a particular person?" I asked.

"I think I've come to a decision that will work." She smiled and it seemed she didn't want to talk about it further. "Did you hear about the commotion in the nearby town?"

"You mean Adams?"

"Yes, the hotel there is teeming with people ever since that nasty newspaper person let the world know that we bought this house. Muckraker is what he is called in polite society."

"Someone told me that he has also come to Adams." I was referring to Annie, who heard it from her friend who worked at the hotel.

She frowned. "You probably don't know this, but Theodore got him fired from the newspaper. Not because of the articles he wrote about us—the editor loved that circulation had increased, but because he had been charging his own meals to the newspaper's expense account. Hah—see how low-minded people are always caught by their own deceptions."

"Mrs. Schaeffer, may I ask you something? Did you do any background checking on the young women who work here?"

"I? No, I worked through an agency in the City. Why do you ask?"

"There's something a little off about them."

She continued to look surprised. "Are they not doing their work?"

"It's not that, it's that they are very vague about who is supposed to do which job and seem to be intentionally confusing Inspector Gladstone."

"What has he got to do with anything?"

"Hasn't he spoken to you about your husband?"

"No," she said even more surprised.

"Never mind," I said. "Can I get you anything?" I asked, standing up.

"No thank you," she answered.

I marched downstairs to see Gladstone still in the morning room, muttering over the notes he had taken earlier.

"Inspector. Have you told Mrs. Schaeffer about her husband's death?"

"Of course. Well, Officer Reed told her."

"No, I mean not that he had died, but how?"

"I thought Tom Reed had done that," he said.

"I don't think she knows. And I'm not going to be the one to tell her. That's your job."

He was startled by my forward comments, but I didn't care. He cleared his throat. "I understood she was too ill…"

"She may be ill, but her mind is working perfectly well. She deserves to hear the truth from you."

He blew out a breath and scratched his head. "You're right. Lead the way."

Shoulders back I walked ahead of him up the stairs to her room and knocking on it slightly, pushed it open, allowing him to go in first.

"I'll be waiting in the hall," I said, abandoning him to his difficult task. I went downstairs to the kitchen instead, fearing she might cry out and I didn't want to hear it. Oh, why did I take this job?

Elsie had gone and the kitchen was quiet. I wondered where the maids were and went through the door that led to the backstairs. I listened but heard no movement. Then I was curious about what 'downstairs' looked like and stepped as quietly as I could manage. There was the lingering smell of whatever it was that Elsie had prepared for dinner as I reached the bottom step. Ahead of me was a long hall with many doors, all closed, and it was dead quiet. I proceeded down the corridor and could see at the end that a door was partially open, and a light shone out.

"Can I help you?" a voice behind me asked.

I gasped, not having heard one of the maids approach me from behind. I put my hand to my chest and said, "You gave me a fright! I was just wondering where everyone was."

"Why?"

"I'm going to be leaving in a little while and wanted to know that someone was ready to look in on Mrs. Schaeffer."

She gave me a hard look behind her glasses. "We have that all sorted out. It's none of your business." She stood almost blocking my way and I tried staring her down.

"Excuse me," I said, and brushed past her, my hand inadvertently touching her side. It was a strange sensation of something thick under the uniform—not fat or flesh—but padding of some kind.

Our eyes met again, and she was glaring at me.

"I'm sorry," I said, wondering what in the world I had encountered as I made my way as fast as possible up the backstairs to the second floor. As I emerged, I could see that Inspector Gladstone was coming out of Mrs. Schaeffer's bedroom and he walked toward me.

"She's a cool customer," he said. "She looked mildly surprised when I told her, not shocked as you might think."

"I have a feeling she didn't like her husband very much. That would explain her reaction."

"Still. To know that someone was murdered in your own house. She might have a maid sleeping in the next room, but whoever could subdue a big man like Mr. Schaeffer would make mincemeat out of one of those girls. Yet they don't seem troubled at all."

"Do they even know his cause of death?" I asked. "If his wife didn't know, what makes you think they do?"

He scratched his head again.

"Maybe now is not the time to tell them, but somebody has an obligation to let them know that they might be living in a dangerous situation."

"Now, Nurse Taylor, I do know my job. I heard talk that he was not a well-liked person and the hotel in Adams is full of folks who had a beef with him. Legitimate or not, it doesn't matter. It had to have been one of those City folks who committed this crime, and it was aimed at a specific person. You notice none of the servants was injured nor was Mrs. Schaeffer."

"Perhaps it was not Mr. Schaeffer who was the intended victim," I said. "Whoever came into the house either knew their way around and which bedroom to go to or in the dark they went to the wrong bedroom."

"Who could have it out for Mrs. Schaeffer?"

I shrugged my shoulders.

"There are two ex-wives, I hear. Maybe they thought she was the tootsie who deposed one of them. Alimony or not, there could be hard feelings about being pushed aside for someone younger," he said.

"But if someone went looking for her bedroom and encountered his instead, they would surely realize almost immediately that it was not a small woman but a big man. That doesn't make sense. But then, nothing makes sense in this house."

One of the maids, not the one I had seen in the basement as far as I could tell, came out through the backstairs door toward us. She was carrying a bundle that looked like pajamas and a bathrobe and I thought she must be the one who was on duty that evening. I nodded to her, and she nodded back and went into Mrs. Schaeffer's room and closed the door.

Chapter 12

It was surprising that two additional hours of work should have made me feel so tired, but it seemed I was a hamster on a wheel trying to keep up with everything. As I drove back down from Highfields, I remembered that it was my night to prepare dinner and I didn't have a clue what was in the refrigerator that could be whipped up into a meal. Guilt washed over me as I thought about how my extended workday was impinging on John's time, too, and wondered how to best deal with all of it.

However, a surprise awaited me when I came into the kitchen from the back door. John swept me in his arms for an enveloping hug, took my coat off and escorted me to the dining room. The table had been set, candles lit, a glass of wine poured, and he pulled the chair out for me.

"Can I change out of my uniform at least?" I asked.

"Not yet." He disappeared back into the kitchen and came back with a roast chicken on a platter, surrounded by potatoes and cabbage.

"Oh, John, it was supposed to be my turn to cook tonight."

"While you were up on millionaire's hill, an angel in the form of Annie appeared with this, knowing that you were working much harder than you should."

"That was sweet of her," I said, suddenly on the verge of tears.

He remained standing to carve the meat and serve the vegetables, giving me a hefty portion.

"I am concerned about you burning the candle at both ends," he said. "You haven't been able to take the afternoon walk that I know rejuvenates you. And you seem preoccupied by the residents of Highfields, even muttering in your sleep."

"Oh, dear. That is troubling."

"We can afford a weekend ski vacation easily enough—it doesn't have to be an entire week at some fancy place. In fact, we're close enough that we can pop up anytime we want."

"I know," I said. "It isn't just that I had my heart set on that particular kind of holiday. I feel sorry for Mrs. Schaeffer, assuming your diagnosis is correct. Her husband referred to her unkindly and now there is this herd of people nearby who had hoped to fix their financial situations with him and will be focused on her instead."

"What do you mean?"

"She's had an attorney in twice that I know of and rewritten her will. Elsie mentioned that there had been a lot of traffic at the front door. Visitors. I didn't get any further details on what that was all about."

I was beginning to relax, having had a substantial taste of the wine. "Where did you get this from, anyway?"

"An appreciative patient. The ever-present Otis dropped it off here when you were gone."

"How did he know where to find you?"

"You're the amateur sleuth. How do you think? He looked at the card posted on the door in the Adams' office that lets everyone know I'm here in the afternoons."

"Still…," I said, concerned that he had popped up. "This chicken is so good, I could never have made a better one."

"Maybe it's time to poach Annie away from Miss Manley."

"You'd better be joking. That would be treason. But if we could magically duplicate her, that would be wonderful. Speaking of duplicates, I was present when Inspector Gladstone was interviewing the maids. They not only look remarkably alike down to the same hairstyle and glasses, I'm sure one of them came in twice pretending to be another." I told him how I had deduced that.

"Must keep one's seams straight!" John said with a laugh.

"It went through my mind that perhaps there are only five maids pretending to be six women. Or maybe there are only four. Who knows? I've never seen them all together. And they were vague about who does what and who was where when Mr. Schaeffer died."

"Aggie, I totally forgot to tell you. The funeral director contacted me and told me when the rigor mortis passed. It seems Mr. Schaeffer could have died much earlier than any of us imagined. Perhaps before five o'clock."

"In the morning?"

"No, in the late afternoon."

"That's not possible. I heard him out in the hall. I heard him talking. He spoke on the telephone."

"I checked very carefully with the funeral director again and asked every pertinent question. Was he sure? Had he stored Mr. Schaeffer's body in a particularly cold room? What else could account for it? I even pored over my medical texts to see if there was anything that could have affected the timing."

I was stunned.

"There are a few factors, however. If exposed to high heat or if he had a fever while alive, rigor would set in more quickly making it seem as if he had died earlier than we thought. If he was very warm before he died or had engaged in exercise, that affects the timing, too."

"His room didn't seem particularly warm when we entered it," I said.

"True, but maybe someone turned the steam heat down. Now keep in mind that the length of time for rigor to pass varies widely, so we can't really extrapolate back to the exact time he passed."

"Except the broken window in the kitchen tells us that it must have happened after I left for the night because it was intact when I went out the kitchen door."

We were silent for a few minutes.

"John, there are several men who had grudges against Mr. Schaeffer. The investor, the newspaper reporter who got fired, the fiancée of an ex-wife, possibly someone associated with the other ex-wife and let's not forget Otis."

"Phew," John said. "If he had that long a list of known enemies, there could be many more that we don't even know about. I'm not happy that Gladstone dragged you into this business even further. I understand your professional duty and empathy toward Mrs. Schaeffer, but if it's getting to be too much, I'm sure we could find a private nurse through my hospital connections in Pittsfield. Someone who could possibly do an eight-hour shift instead of relying on maids 'looking in on her', as her husband described it, with you as a two-hour evening distraction. I don't think she's getting the proper attention or care."

"Normally, I would react by jumping up and saying, I can do it! But I think you're right. Why don't you call Doctor Schell in Pittsfield and I'll broach the topic with Mrs. Schaeffer. Despite your best efforts at getting her to move around, I can see she is fading away. Not eating much, lying in bed all day from what I have heard, and at her age, that's not good."

"I'm glad you understand. We must keep her best interests in mind. And something close to round-the-clock care at this point would be a good idea. Lord knows she can afford it."

"I have an even better suggestion. Let's forget all about them for the rest of the evening. After we finish dinner, why don't we listen to the radio or play cards? Anything to get our minds off the problems of others?"

"Excellent idea," John said. He held his glass up. "And we'll have that ski vacation, no matter what."

Chapter 13

The next morning, John said I still looked tired and allowed me to sleep in, which turned out to be not very long as I could hear him crashing around in the kitchen. I came downstairs in my bathrobe to see what was going on and he looked startled.

"I was looking for the waffle iron," he said. "You know the electric one that Miss Ballantine gave us."

"Why?" seemed a logical question.

"I was going to make you some waffles, of course."

I filled the coffee pot with water, the basket with grounds and put it on the stove.

"Let's save that for the weekend. I think making them will be more time-consuming than you imagine and you don't want to be late this morning."

He shrugged and I took eggs from the refrigerator and two slices of ham.

"If you're going to cook, then I'll call Doctor Schell." He went into the hallway to the telephone and had a conversation about the

Schaeffer situation and the requirements and said he could not comment on the pay but that it was likely to be generous.

"He's got someone in mind and said he would send her over during your shift this evening," he said when he returned. "But first, I'd better talk to Mrs. Schaeffer and let her know that it is my recommendation for the sake of her health."

Although I didn't get to sleep in, it was nice not to have to watch the clock while getting ready, and I could be dressed casually for the morning at least. I took my time and decided to walk into town, get some bread and stop by the post office to replenish our stamp supply.

It was a cold but sunny morning, and the snow on the ground was only about an inch deep, no trouble for me in my trusty fur-lined boots. They had been suitable for the New York City weather where the streets were quickly plowed and the sidewalks shoveled. I had learned the hard way the previous winter in West Adams that, while fashionable, they were no match for the deep snow and so I had knee-high, lace-up boots for any forays in the countryside.

It was relaxing to take my time walking past the houses on the main street before crossing into the more commercial part of town and seeing familiar faces that I didn't usually encounter except in John's office.

I said hello to Mrs. Hancock outside the hardware store.

"Well, it looks like you've got the morning off," she said with a smile.

"I know. That taskmaster doctor I work for is letting me out for a stroll."

She thought that was very funny.

I saw Miss Olsen, whom I would have expected to be in Pittsfield with Mrs. Proctor, but she told me that she was on a constituent errand and made it seem confidential and important, so I didn't pursue it. Since her appointment as an assistant to one of the County Commissioners and the salary that went with it, she wore a smart wool suit under an expensive camel hair coat that must have been purchased in Pittsfield, if not in Hartford. I felt a pang of envy since I wore my uniform every day but then remembered how much money I saved by not having to buy new outfits every season as the fashions changed.

Some of the shops had Christmas decorations up and I was beginning to wonder what I should get John. Probably a warm sweater would be the best gift and I might have to drive over to Pittsfield to find something appropriate; the store in West Adams sold work clothes such as flannel shirts, hats with ear flaps and steel-toed shoes. Adams had a men's store, but since we walked past it every day, it wouldn't be much of a surprise for him to know I bought the blue sweater that had been in the window for weeks. If we went down to Pelham for Christmas, I would be sure to go into the City where there was a multitude of choices.

"Excuse me," said a voice at my elbow that startled me out of my thoughts. It was a young man with his collar turned up and a hat pulled down over his ears, seeming to lack the appropriate clothing for a December day even if the sun was shining. I thought he was about to ask me for a handout. "Are you Nurse Taylor?"

"Yes, I am," I answered hesitantly.

"Ken Stafford," he said, sticking out an ungloved hand by way of introduction.

"Nice to meet you," I said, wondering who he was and how he knew who I was.

I smiled and continued walking.

"May I talk with you for a few moments?"

My wary New York instincts took over. "What about?"

"I understand that you are working up at the Schaeffers' house."

I said nothing.

"Is that true?" he persisted.

"Who are you and why do you want to know?"

"I work for the **Knickerbocker News** in Manhattan and I...."

"No, you don't," I said.

That stopped him short and the look in his eye told me he was about to brazen it out but smiled conspiratorially instead. "You're right. I used to work there. I'm freelance now, a stringer for the **Hartford News**."

"What's a stringer?" I had never heard the term before.

"I pick up a story and write about it and then pitch it to them. If they run it, I get paid."

"That doesn't sound like a reliable way to make a living." I walked away, but he continued to follow me.

"Is it true that Mr. Schaeffer was killed by his wife?"

I spun around to face him. "Leave me alone," I said and walked into the post office. Unbelievably, he followed me inside and was only inches from my elbow.

The postmaster could sense that something was wrong, and we greeted one another as if there was not some person leaning in toward me and pestering me with questions.

"Mrs. Taylor, is this man bothering you?" the postmaster asked, drilling a threatening look over his wire rim glasses at the reporter.

"Yes, he is, but I am doing my best to ignore him."

"I would be happy to call Officer Reed if you think that's necessary."

I turned to look at the stringer next to me and said, "If he takes one step closer or asks me one more question, I may lose my temper. And I think everybody in town knows what that could look like." It was a total bluff since I rarely lost my temper and certainly nobody in West Adams had ever seen it in full force. But it worked its magic and the reporter stepped away.

"You people are all alike. Circle the wagons when one of you is threatened. Theodore Schaeffer was the worst excuse for a human being, and you all conspired to protect him from his past deeds."

"Most of us never met the man," said the postmaster.

"I have no idea what you're talking about," I said, although I did. But I wasn't going to share what I had overheard or what gossip had circulated about the man. I turned back and completed my postal transaction and began to walk out with the reporter still following me.

I turned on him again. "Get out of my way and stop following me," I said in my Head Nurse Watson voice.

Finally, he backed away, hunched further into his suit jacket as he prepared to exit onto the cold street. The postmaster winked at me in approval.

"That man has been making a pest of himself all over town asking all sorts of foolish questions. He actually expected me to tell him what mail the Schaeffers received!"

"That's an insult to your professionalism," I said stoutly.

"Indeed."

My transaction finished, I peered out the window to see if the reporter was lying in wait, but he had disappeared. The street was unusually busy for a cold morning, but that only meant that people walked more briskly, some with heads down against a strong wind that seemed to bluster down the main street from the woods above.

I stopped in the bakery for a fresh loaf of white bread, then the grocer's for green beans and hurried back home, wishing I had worn a warmer scarf. The rest of my morning was pottering around the house, dusting before sitting down at the dining table to begin the task of personalizing the Christmas cards that I had purchased in Adams the week before. I heard John come in through the back door to the kitchen and called out to him.

"Ah, the season is upon us already?" he asked.

"How could you possibly not notice? There are decorations in a lot of the stores already, and every good husband has been devoting endless hours to finding the perfect gift for his wife."

"Of course!" he said, taking off his overcoat. "It feels like snow."

"It feels like the Arctic, I think."

"I found someone to help with Mrs. Schaeffer," he said. "What's for lunch?" he was already back in the kitchen, rubbing his hands together.

"I just got some fresh bread, and your favorite ham and cheese awaits. Along with some special mustard that one of the patients dropped off."

He put his head around the corner to catch my eye. "Who makes mustard?"

I shrugged. "I guess someone grows mustard plants around here, but I haven't opened the card that came along with the jar to see."

"You want a sandwich, too?"

"Yes, thank you," I said, putting the cards into a stack for John to add his signature, and joined him in the kitchen.

"It's from Mr. Reilly. And it's really good. Taste." He put a bit on a spoon for me to try,

"Wow, that's spicy. Just as you like it. Tell me about whom you found to help."

"Her name is Pauline Watson and she'll be showing up this afternoon. She does night duty at the hospital in Pittsfield."

"Does she plan on doing both? Eight hours there and another eight at Highfields? That's a stretch."

"I brought up the issue of lack of sleep and she said she only needs five hours."

"Well, good for her," I said, never quite believing when people bragged about how little rest they needed. I hoped she didn't think part of her sleeping time was at one of the two jobs.

Our afternoon in West Adams was busy with sore throats, a possible strep throat, chilblains, some poor woman we'd never seen before who was losing her hair and thought the doctor could do something about it. After some questioning, he discovered that she had given birth only a few weeks before and was surprised to find out that some hair loss was natural with all the hormonal changes. When he told her, she began to cry, then to laugh at herself, confirming the diagnosis.

Just as she left, another woman came in wearing a nurse's cap. "Boston General?"

I inquired, pointing at her cap since the style of cap was indicative of where one had trained.

"Yes, and you?"

I told her where I had been in Manhattan, and she gave a whistle of appreciation.

"You must be Pauline," I said. "I'm Aggie."

I liked the looks of her. She was average height but strongly built and had bright red hair pulled back off her collar in a knot at the back of her head. There was something about her no-nonsense look that reassured me that she would be up to the strange task of working for Mrs. Schaeffer, which hardly seemed like work to me.

Since there was no one else in the reception room, I helped her out of her overcoat and asked her to sit down so I could fill her in on some of the particulars of what might be expected.

John came out from his office and introduced himself and held his hand palm up in my direction, giving me the floor.

"Mrs. Schaeffer is very ill and has been for some time. She doesn't need to be lifted or carried but does need some assistance in walking as she is getting weaker and may be wobbly."

"How old is she?"

"Only thirty-eight," I said, and Pauline winced.

"She's in that big house on the hill with a raft of servants, none of whom has any medical training as far as I can tell. One of them sleeps in the room next to her but there is very little supervision of Mrs. Schaeffer during the day. They 'look in on her' from time to time as they put it."

"Gosh, that sounds terrible. Is there a Mr. Schaeffer?"

"There used to be, but he recently passed away."

"That's too bad."

John interjected, "I should tell you it seems he was killed in his bed."

Her eyes grew wide. "In that house? Where I'm supposed to work?" She began to get up, and I put my hand on her arm while glaring at John's comment.

"It appears someone broke into the house. We understand that her husband was very unpopular with a lot of people."

"Are we talking gangsters or something?" She looked from me to John.

"No, he was very wealthy from business deals. I've never got the full story from his wife about what sort of work he did, but there is at least one angry gentleman who came up from the City to confront him about something from his past."

"Oh," she said, somewhat mollified and sitting down again.

"And at least one ex-wife who hoped to get a raise in her alimony payments."

"Interesting."

"But they can't have any grudge against his wife. At least, nobody has mentioned her in all this mess. And they must know that she is seriously ill."

"Isn't there security at the house?"

"There is as of today, I understand. I'm there from five until seven each night, mostly to keep her company and she's got someone nearby all night. It's the daytime hours where she could be better supervised."

Pauline got up again. "I'm not ready to make a commitment yet, but game to meet her if you'll show me the way to the house."

It was not yet three o'clock, so I took Glenda's car and had Pauline follow me in hers after instructing her that it was not that far away. As we wound up the driveway to Highfields, I looked in the rearview mirror to catch her expression, which was one of astonishment. I guess John hadn't told her the extent of the property, but she was certainly as impressed as I had been the first time I saw the house and grounds and the spectacular view of Mount Greylock in the distance.

I motioned her to park at the back of the house near the kitchen entrance and we came into the warm room with the delicious smells of Elsie's cooking. I introduced them and said that I would take Pauline up to meet the patient after giving her a brief tour of the downstairs.

"Whatever business he was in must have done very well. I'm surprised any millionaires made it through the Crash with any money." She looked around at the wood-paneled walls. "What a place to keep up."

"The maids—there are six of them, I think—come and go carrying things."

She shot me an amused look. "No cleaning or dusting or anything?"

"I've never seen it, but I'm only here in the evening and only started this week myself. There must be some folks who'll come in to do deep cleaning sometime. I suppose," I added.

"The maids sleep on the third floor and there are rooms in the basement where they eat and maybe do additional work, like polishing silver." I was making it up as I went along.

I took her down the hall and gestured to the study, and she looked in and waved her hand in front of her face. "Cigars?"

"Yes, the smoke lingers a long time."

We ascended the massive staircase and I let her know there were bedrooms behind the closed doors as well as an entry to the back stairs that went from the basement up to the attic.

"Mrs. Schaeffer's room," I said as I knocked briefly on the door.

She lay in bed with a fashion magazine propped open in her lap. "You're early," she said before noticing Pauline behind me. "Who's this?"

"Pauline Watson, ma'am. I understood that you were looking for additional help during the day."

"Just so. Come, tell me about yourself." She patted the side of the bed, and they began a conversation that was more of a chat than a job interview, but it seemed to be the way that Mrs. Schaeffer liked to do things.

I tidied the nightstands, looked into the bathroom to make sure that everything she might need was available. Passing in front of the windows that overlooked the driveway, I thought I saw a man looking up at the house, but a pine tree partially obscured my view. A moment later, the man stepped out onto the driveway and I saw it was the reporter, but he quickly shot out of view when a car approached. I could hear Inspector Gladstone's voice calling after the retreating figure through the open driver's side window. He evidently gave up and shut off the motor, turned off the lights and walked around to the front door.

"Excuse me," I said, leaving not to answer the door, as surely there were enough maids about, but to see what it was that Gladstone wanted. I stood at the top of the stairs and saw him approach. The maid who had let him in slid off to a side room. I went down the stairs to inquire.

"I thought you were done here," I remarked.

"And I thought you didn't come to work until five o'clock."

"I brought along another nurse who may put in some hours attending to Mrs. Schaeffer."

"Is she that bad?"

"She's very sick," I said, the usual vague response about someone obviously in serious decline.

"I thought she had hired a security person," he said. "I don't think that's who it was who scurried into the bushes."

"I don't know where that man is—I've yet to meet him. This is a big property and maybe he thinks his job is to check out the perimeter of the grounds rather than stand guard duty at the doors. I think the person you saw was the reporter from New York who alerted the world that Mr. Schaeffer had bought this house in the first place. I understand that Mr. Schaeffer did him a good turn and had him fired."

Gladstone shook his head at the intrigue. "I'm here to interview the six pretty maids all in a row. And I mean to have them come in all at once and I'll get to the bottom of what they're up to."

"Did you ever locate the employment agency some of them referred to?" I asked, thinking that was a logical place to start.

"No, I didn't. It might very well exist, but a call to a Manhattan operator did not yield any results." He took off his overcoat and gloves and put them on a chair.

"There are five boroughs in New York City, you know. Maybe the agency was in Brooklyn or—"

He cut me off. "I am aware that the City is big. There is only so much time I can devote to figuring out who these girls are or where they came from. Officer Reed and I have had our hands full with the folks at the Adams hotel. The two ex-wives, number two who replaced number one, had nothing but hateful things to say about him and each other. One thing they agree upon is that now Mr. Schaeffer is gone, that's the end of the dole for them. In other words, they could not possibly have any reason to kill the goose who continued to lay the golden eggs."

"Except revenge. That's a powerful motive."

He looked at me sharply. "You're right. It's sometimes more powerful than greed."

"That former business partner or investor had an axe to grind, as well," I said.

"What I don't understand is why all of them are still here. You would think once the old man was gone, they would scatter, especially if they thought they might be considered suspects."

"Did you or Officer Reed tell them not to leave town?"

"No. I interviewed each one of them and got what I could out of them. Which was not much. It was more a recitation of past grievances and character assassination. Maybe they think they can persuade Mrs. Schaeffer to make good their financial losses."

I let out a laugh. "They can't be serious. Why would she want to do that?"

He shrugged.

"You don't suspect the staff here, do you?"

"Certainly not. I've run out of suspects and motives. I just don't like it that they tried to pull the wool over my eyes, and I mean to shake them up a bit. Somebody must have seen or heard something. I think that business of needing to have a woman present was a lot of nonsense to confuse things. I just asked what's-her-name who let me in to call the rest of the Girl Scouts down for a line up."

I couldn't imagine what good that would do but decided to go back up to see how Pauline was faring. As I mounted the stairs, I could see six sullen figures, all alike, walking in a line into the morning room, Inspector Gladstone with his hands on his hips surveying them. They slunk past him as if he had a sap in his hand that he intended to use on them.

Pauline and Mrs. Schaeffer seemed to have got on like a house on fire, chatting and giggling over something in the magazine as I came in.

"Inspector Gladstone is here talking to the maids," I said.

Mrs. Schaeffer's face fell. "Again? Why does he keep pestering them?"

"Well, they were here that night. And they gave him some vague answers that only inflamed him into thinking he might need to double down to find out if they heard or saw anything. They'll be fine. They're a lot sharper than they let on."

She looked at me quizzically. "Pauline, I'd like you to stay until Nurse Taylor comes back, let's say five-thirty tonight?"

"That would be fine," I said, knowing that I could catch the tea group gathering before having to return here.

I didn't need to go out the front way when I left, but I made a point of getting close enough to the morning room door where the inquisition was taking place. I could hear the frustration in Gladstone's voice as he said, "Wait a minute, you said Jane was the one who answered the telephone."

"I never said that. It was Ann who must have said so," one of the girls said.

"What's going on here?" He practically yelled.

"I told you they were liars," another voice said.

That broke the tension and they all started talking at once, accusing one another of making up stories, calling each other names, and it sounded as if there was going to be an all-out brawl in a moment. In the midst of all that racket, I walked into the room and clapped my hands for silence, just as Head Nurse Watson would have done.

"That's enough! There's a sick woman in the house and plenty of work for you all to be doing."

Every one of them turned to look at me with intense dislike and without another word, they filed out of the room as they had come in, leaving Gladstone behind.

Chapter 14

I couldn't wait to get out into the cold air and away from the chaos inside. But I forgotten that I had parked around the back of the house and had to circle back to my car. A large shape loomed in the darkness.

"Miss?"

I yelped.

"It's only me, Jim. I'm working security."

When he stepped out into the light that streamed from the house's windows, I recognized him as one of the local farmers' sons, probably hired because he had nothing much else to do in the winter. Standing out in the cold didn't seem to be a very effective way of providing security and I wondered if that was once again Mrs. Schaeffer's hiring technique at work.

"There was a man out here earlier," I said.

"That was Inspector Gladstone," he said.

"I know, but there was someone else, too. I think it was that New York reporter. He's probably snooping around for some story he hopes to cook up to redeem his sullied reputation." I could tell that Jim had no idea what I was talking about, and I didn't have time to explain.

"I'm going back into town, but I'll be back by five-thirty. Are you going to be out here all night?" I asked.

"No, my brother is going to spell me later."

I walked along the drive to where Glenda's car was parked, keeping well away from the bushes, concerned that someone else would come popping out now that it was getting dark. Over the long summer I'd forgotten how sunset was so early in December, especially when it disappeared behind the mountains.

Miss Manley's house was lit up and I was one of many just arriving, although by habit I came in the back door to the kitchen, even hanging my coat up on the hooks laden with gardening hats and jackets. I had brought my tote bag with shoes in it to change out of my warm but slightly wet boots, a hazard of winter in the Berkshires where you needed at least two pairs of boots, one drying and one about to get wet.

The chatter in the sitting room was lively with discussions about the Christmas recital at the local school, the manger display in front of the church, and what the most popular toys would be for young children. That made me even more aware that I hadn't solidified our Christmas plans—whether to stay up in West Adams or to go down to Pelham. Some of that depended on Glenda and Stuart who might want to enjoy a white Christmas with Aunt Manley. If they needed to stay in the City, she could be with them or if we went to Pelham to visit my parents, she could bunk with us. Being married with more family was more complicated than my life used to be, where I could just pick up and go and not think about others' expectations so much.

Annie had outdone herself with a variety of holiday-themed cookies: candy cane shapes with white and red icing, Christmas trees with tiny jimmies looking like ornaments and acorn cookies, maple-flavored ovals half dipped in chocolate and sprinkled with nuts.

There was a flurry when Mrs. Proctor and Miss Olsen came in and I was hoping we were not going to suffer through another diatribe about public policy and politics. But it was Miss Olsen who was flushed and dying to share her news. She held her left hand out proudly.

"I'm engaged!"

There were gasps and congratulations and I could hardly hear when the obvious question of 'who's the lucky man' was answered. It turned out I didn't recognize the name, but some of the others did and knew he had a legal practice in Pittsfield, which boded well for her future. Even if she chose not to work after marriage—although by the stern look on Mrs. Proctor's face that decision hadn't been settled—she would be living in the more vibrant Pittsfield.

"You'd better not forget about us," someone chided.

"How could I? My family still lives here. I'll be back and forth all the time."

Miss Ballantine was anxious to know if there was going to be a tree lighting ceremony as there was a large fir tree near what used to be the town green, once a place where people used to park their wagons before the advent of automobiles.

"Why not?" Mrs. Rockmore asked. "It's only lit for a few hours each night and we all enjoy the children singing Christmas carols as it's done."

"We could have a bonfire, too," Miss Ballantine suggested.

"Isn't that a little heathen?" Nina whispered to me with a chuckle in her voice.

"Does that mean we'll have to dance around the fire and sacrifice someone?" I asked in a low tone to her in response.

Mrs. Proctor shot me a look that told me whispering was not to be encouraged in this group. It made me think about the times I had been called out for talking to my best friend in class and I had to suppress a smile.

The telephone rang and Miss Manley looked over at me for assistance since she was boxed in behind the tea service table at that moment.

"I'll get it," I said, maneuvering around the chairs through the hall to the kitchen where the old-fashioned phone hung on the wall. I picked up the earpiece and spoke into the mouthpiece, an awkward position for me since the device had been mounted on the wall for Miss Manley who was considerably shorter.

"Aggie? Is that you? Why are you answering the phone?"

"Tea group," I said, not wanting my voice to be carried down the hall and into the sitting room.

"For a moment I thought maybe John had kicked you out already for burning the toast."

She laughed merrily at what I thought was a stupid joke. She was the one who couldn't boil water. "I guess I called at a bad time. I wanted to know her plans for Christmas. We're wavering between going up there, where things will be peaceful and boring, or bringing her down here where there will be plays, dinners and cocktail parties."

"Do you think she would enjoy that? Or are you angling to have her babysit Douglas while you and Stuart paint the town?"

"Aggie! What a thing to say. But now that you mention it, what a good idea! I know she'd enjoy the shop windows on Fifth Avenue and the men with roasted chestnuts on the corners. Stuart actually wants to take Douglas sledding in Central Park, but he's much too young. And there's not enough snow yet, anyway."

"When it does snow, he could tow him on a sled. I bet he'd find that fun." That was most of the sledding we did as children as there weren't enough steep hills to go down that weren't peppered with giant boulders. My brother tried it once and that was the end of his sled.

"What's going on up there at Highfields?" Glenda asked.

"What do you mean?"

"I heard that horrible Mr. Schaeffer died. Now what will happen to the house?"

"How do you know he was horrible?"

"He used to own some clothing manufacturing firm in lower Manhattan. They call it the 'rag trade' down here although he was a partner in one that was very high end. A friend of mine knows a girl who was a showroom model—you know, they come out in the new designs so the customers can see how they look on an actual body, not on a hanger."

"Yes, like the way the rest of us shop," I said.

"Anyway, he was well known for taking more than a little interest in some of them. The girl I heard about not only got fired but was blackballed. No one else would hire here."

"Ugh. Are you sure?"

"I gather she wasn't the only one."

"I do know that the current Mrs. Schaeffer is wife number three. That's common knowledge, not gossip," I clarified. "Although I don't think she was one of the showroom models."

"Anyway, please ask my aunt to call me so we can discuss plans."

I entered the sitting room to our hostess's inquiring glance and, as I was trying to figure out how to mime the content of the conversation, gave up, leaned over and whispered in Miss Manley's ear that Glenda requested a call back.

The eyes of Mrs. Proctor were on me again, so I stood up straight and announced to the group that Glenda had just called and wanted to know Miss Manley's plans for Christmas. "Oh, and I have to go home and then to work. Good evening, ladies."

Only Mrs. Proctor and Miss Manley caught the sarcasm in my voice as several women said goodnight at my departure. That woman had let the electoral power go to her head, I thought. I slipped out the back door, across the backyard and then to our house, entering through the reception door to the office as the light was still on.

"Hi, just checking in before my next shift," I said to John, who was in his office.

"Are you going like that? With a smear of chocolate on your face?"

I had to laugh and looked at myself in the small mirror on the wall. "Oops. No wonder my scathing exit line didn't have its intended effect."

"I was just up at Highfields. Pauline called and said she thought Mrs. Schaeffer was in considerable pain."

"Oh, dear."

"I gave her a shot of morphine. That's about all we can do at this point."

"She seems to have diminished so quickly," I said.

"In the final analysis, that's probably a good thing. No need to have her suffer."

I put my arms around him and held him tightly. "As far as I know, she has no family. And she doesn't know anybody here except me and you and her new friend Pauline."

"It might be a good idea for the two of you to stay there all day in shifts. This nonsense of a maid being in an adjacent room is not going to be of any use if she needs medical attention."

The reception door opened and a thunderous looking Inspector Gladstone stormed in. "Why didn't you tell me about all these people?" he said as he came across the room.

"What people?" John asked.

"Your face is very red. Are you all right?" I asked.

"No, I'm not. I'm boiling mad because Officer Reed has the flu and I have to handle this entire mess by myself. And I just found out that you had talked to one of the ex-wives."

"Yes. But it was a medical matter, if you must know. She was in the attorneys' offices in Adams, and she evidently fainted and bumped her head. We brought her down the hall to my office until she was well enough to leave."

"What did she tell you?"

"Not much. It was her fiancé who complained about Theodore Schaeffer and that her alimony wasn't enough for her to live on. She intended to petition either him or the court to increase it."

"That's ridiculous. They probably got married and divorced in New York. So why is she talking to an attorney up here?"

John shrugged. "I got the feeling Mr. Schaeffer was feeling the heat from too many people in the City and went to a bolthole up here."

"Who's this fiancé person?"

John looked at me. "Johnson? Was that his name?"

"I think it was Johnstone."

"He could be a major suspect," Gladstone said.

"That's true, based on the tone of his comments. But if Mr. Schaeffer died, there would be no more alimony paid. So, it would be a stupid thing for him to do."

"Wasn't there another ex-wife floating around? And did she, too, come to confer with you and you didn't tell me?"

"No," I said in a haughty tone.

"But we did hear from the dentist Doctor English upstairs that one of Schaeffer's former business partners had come up here from New

York on some kind of legal mission. Plenty of suspects," John said calmly.

"If anyone else comes to you with a tale to tell, send them directly to me next time," the inspector said. He gave me a hard look and stomped out.

"Why does he talk to you as if you are a misbehaving subordinate?" John asked.

"Maybe it's because I'm able to get people to talk and all he does is scare the daylights out of them."

Chapter 15

It seemed I hadn't been home very long before having to set out again. At least now there was someone else up at the house to look after Mrs. Schaeffer's needs. I drove carefully on the way up the hill, aware that there might be icy patches, and found the house lit up as if every room were in use.

Elsie was in high dudgeon muttering to the stovetop when I entered the kitchen. She turned her head at my approach to make sure it was me without missing a beat in stirring whatever was in the pot.

"Nobody tells me anything," she said. "Two of the maids just took off. It's not my business if they leave and never come back, but there's all this food that was delivered and I cooked not knowing there would be only four of them."

"Maybe Jim could help you out. He looks like he has a healthy appetite."

She turned a rueful smile on me. "I shouldn't be complaining. It's just hard when things change so quickly. When I worked for the Lewises, I was out to the shops, seeing my friends, having a cup of coffee with Annie. And Mrs. Lewis would chat with me as we worked on a project together. This place is so lonesome since I'm stuck in the kitchen from noon until I leave, and nobody talks to me."

I didn't want to say it, but due to Mrs. Schaeffer's health, it was likely that the job was not going to last beyond the end of the month.

"Here, have a biscuit, fresh from the oven," she said.

She was an excellent cook and now I could see how those maids had the identical square-looking bodies. So would I if I had this food at every meal.

"I'll let Pauline know I'm here first, then come back down for a chat."

I went upstairs in the quiet house and saw my nursing counterpart was sitting by a sleeping Mrs. Schaeffer. I nodded and pointed to my watch indicating I'd be back shortly. I tiptoed out of the room and came face to face with one of the remaining maids. I hadn't heard her approach. She nodded and made for the backstairs.

It was in that moment that I replayed the events of the night that Mr. Schaeffer died—although there was still no consensus on the exact time. I had made a terrible mistake in not being clear with Inspector Gladstone that I never actually saw Mr. Schaeffer that night. I heard heavy footsteps in the hall. Then the phone rang and one of the maids told him about the call and he muttered something.

What if it wasn't Mr. Schaeffer at all out in the hall? It could have been someone else—the fiancé or the swindled investor. But how would they have known one of the maids well enough to orchestrate such a charade? Had the murder been so well-planned in advance that they counted on me as a reliable witness to swear that I had heard his approach and his reply? I even said that I smelled the cigar smoke from his study as I went down the stairs. That was entirely true. But anybody could have lit a cigar and swirled the smoke around in the air or just left it burning in an ashtray.

One of the maids by herself could have created the illusion of there being a heavy-set man approaching the room that night and then made it seem that a conversation had taken place. After all, it was just a muttered phrase that I heard, not any words. Then she or another maid could have stomped off, making us on the other side of the bedroom door think that he had gone back downstairs to talk on the telephone.

That's why when they were interviewed, they were so vague about whose job it was to answer the phone as well as who was where at any given time. Was Mr. Schaeffer already dead

when I was there, and had I been purposefully put there to substantiate somebody's alibi that he was still alive? Again, who had access or a relationship with one of the maids to perpetrate the crime? And if he were already dead when I was there, which was a possibility, then the broken window in the kitchen was just a subterfuge to make it seem that there had been a break-in and an unknown assailant was responsible, not someone already in the house.

The answer lay with the maids, and I was determined to find out their relationship to whoever did this deed. Forgoing the biscuit that awaited me downstairs, I went to the back stairway behind a closed door and quietly went up the stairs. It was silent and I took my time, not wanting to startle anyone. As I came up to the top of the stairs, I could see that there were several rooms with the doors open and I was bold enough to put my head around the corner of the nearest one to observe a remarkable sight.

There on the bed, sitting cross-legged and mending a stocking, was a slim girl with blonde hair that tumbled past her shoulders. Who was this? Had she been hiding in plain sight all this while and someone smuggled food up to her?

I must have made a sound because she looked up and narrowed her eyes at me.

"What do you want?" she asked.

I approached more slowly and took in the fact that there was a wig sitting on the small dresser. A brown wig. And if you were to put that wig on the slim girl, a pair of glasses, a maid's uniform—padded out to make her look stout—she could pass for any of the six whom we regularly saw.

"Who are you? Or rather, which one are you?" I asked.

She didn't reply but whistled and behind me appeared two of the maids in their usual garb and another one, wigless, who grabbed me by the arms and propelled me into the room.

The girl on the bed held up a pair of scissors and looked menacingly at me.

"What do you know?"

"Nothing, I guess. I thought you all looked remarkably similar, but I didn't think it was an active disguise until now." The door closed behind me.

"We had to look alike, lumpy and undesirable. It was protection against *him*. We knew what he was capable of."

At that moment the snippet of conversation about his behavior with his female employees came to the forefront of my consciousness. Could that have been a motive for murder?

"Sit down," she commanded, and I sat on the only chair in the room, a hardbacked wooden chair. She nodded to one of the others who left the room, returning with a clothesline. I automatically tensed up in anticipation.

No, they weren't going to tie me up, were they?

That's exactly what they did.

"I'd put a gag in your mouth, but nobody would hear you up here yelling. Damn, I thought we could get out of here tomorrow, but it looks like you've pushed our departure ahead significantly. Oh, well."

"You're going to miss some excellent biscuits that Elsie made for dinner."

"Keep yapping and I'll find that sock," she replied.

The others disappeared and I could hear them rummaging around in bureaus and closets, probably packing what little they had brought. This one calmly did the same, hauling a small suitcase out of the closet and jamming clothes into it from the chest behind her.

"Which one are you?" I asked.

"Take your pick. Jane or June, Nan or Ann, Bess or Beth. We're all alike, automatons, interchangeable servants."

"How did you come to be here? Who hired you?"

"You've asked enough questions," she said. "I may be tempted to put find a dirty sock so I don't have to hear any more. Uppity, nosy nurse."

I may have been nosy all right, but I didn't consider myself uppity.

"Here's the deal," she said, snapping the latches on the suitcase as she put her outdoor shoes on her feet. "You're going to stay up here quietly and comfortably, and once we get to a telephone, we'll call the house and tell whoever answers to untie you." She looked me over once again. "No, on second thought, I'll let them find you in due time. Someone is bound to come up here snooping, just as you did." She gave me one last, disgusted look as she put on her overcoat and a hat.

"You won't get away with this, you know."

"Oh, yes, we will. A worthless slug has been taken out of the world and Mrs. Schaeffer can pass away in peace. Nobody cares about us —nobody knows who we are." She left and closed the door behind her, so sure that she was safe that she didn't bother to lock the door.

I could hear them conferring in low tones in the corridor and then they softly walked down the stairs and probably out into the dark night, never to be seen again.

Chapter 16

I thought it best to wait some minutes to make sure they were really and truly gone before I started to think how I was going to get out of my crude prison. Clothesline, indeed. What did the heroines in silent movies do when tied to the railroad tracks?

Wait for the hero to come rescue them.

That wasn't going to happen.

I was secured by my torso to the back of the ladder chair, my hands fastened in front of me with a different piece of rope and my feet tied together. I guessed I could try to hop along the floor to the door and shout out of the keyhole, but the door to the backstairs was typically closed and Pauline would not be able to hear me. If only Elsie thought to rescue me with a biscuit in hand.

At first, I hadn't realized that by tensing up when they had applied the rope that my chest had expanded and now, in a slightly more relaxed mode, the binding felt slacker. It was loose enough that, by wriggling my torso and shoulders, I was able to move it ever so slightly upwards. It took a lot of effort and a woman with a larger bust than I would have been in trouble. I was almost out of breath when many minutes later, the first loop of rope slipped over the top rung of the chair and then the rest came up easily. At least my upper body was freed.

I glanced at my watch and saw I had been at this for at least twenty minutes. The maids were easily down into the town, but if they wanted to make good their escape, they would have to have caught the last bus to Pittsfield. They probably did. And then scatter—and in their real clothes and natural hair, no one would be able to identify them as the culprits.

I started to work at the bonds on my hands with my teeth, the best tool I had available. It was obvious the girl who tied me up had not taken a sailing class; these were very simple knots to undo. My fingers were the obvious tools to loosen the ropes from my ankles and I was soon standing and rubbing my sore wrists. Who were these young women? Avenging angels who had suffered from Mr. Schaeffer's advances and taken their revenge? What had they to do with any of the other people who had trekked up to the Berkshires to have it out with the man?

I walked through the unlocked door and checked each of the maids' rooms to make sure no one was still there. The bedclothes were in a mess and the closet doors open, but otherwise, there was nothing of value to see. No explanatory note, no missing map. They were just gone.

Making my way quickly downstairs, I saw Pauline emerging from Mrs. Schaeffer's room.

"I was just about to go downstairs to see if you had come yet. What were you doing upstairs?"

"The technical term is snooping, and I was rewarded by finding out that none of those girls look anything like they had presented themselves. They wore wigs and phony glasses and some of them padded themselves out to appear stouter and somehow more similar."

She stared at me. "Whatever for?"

"I'm not sure why they wore disguises, but two of them left earlier and the other four skedaddled about half an hour ago."

"Should we call the police? Did they take anything?"

"Not that I know of. How is Mrs. Schaeffer?"

"She's awake and very weak. I was about to go down and get her some tea. I was thinking I might need to call Doctor Taylor about another pain shot."

"I'll go sit with her," I said. "But not a word about the disappearing maids. Not just yet."

I knocked on the door and went in to see her frail body in the bed but a luminous smile on her face.

"You seem very perky this evening," I said.

"Yes, I'm feeling much better. Pauline is good company. Not that you aren't," she added.

"I'm sorry I left my cane and top hat back home or I would do a little song and dance for you."

"That's what got me into all this," she said. I was surprised that she wanted to talk, but once begun there was no stopping her.

"I was dancing in a revue on Broadway when I caught Theodore's eye. Everyone hastened to tell me all the terrible things he had done, who he had cheated, the two wives he had left behind. You know what? I didn't care. I had to leave school at fourteen to help support the family and worked my entire life. Why not marry such a man as long as he could keep me fed and clothed and comfortable. I was almost thirty when we met and I didn't relish being a hoofer much longer. Neither did the producers who did the hiring, and you can't keep pretending to be twenty-five forever." She shrugged her shoulders. "It wasn't so bad. Until I got sick."

I couldn't imagine having to face such a choice, but my profession was always in demand and didn't depend upon how high I could kick my leg or tap out a cadence. Nursing also had the advantage of being a respectable way for a woman to make a living, as I knew folks often looked down upon performers, women in particular.

"Pauline has gone down to get some tea. Would you like to play cards?"

"That would be fun. Do you know how to play Eights?"

"No," I said.

"Oh, good. Then I might be able to win. Let me explain the rules. You deal out eight cards to each for us, put the rest in the stockpile and then turn one over. From your hand, you must match either the number on the card or the suit. If you can't, you draw from the deck. But, if you have an eight in your hand, you can play it and designate the suit. Easy."

"All right, I said, pulling a chair next to the bed and dealing the cards out onto the tray table that sat across her lap.

"I'll go first," she said.

She looked at the card that was face up, drew a card from the deck and discarded it quickly.

"I have to tell you the funniest thing that happened today. I got a call from a young man who claims to be Theodore's son." She laughed.

"Why is that funny?"

"Don't you think it strange that he should wait until his father dies to pop up out of nowhere and declare himself the heir?"

"Yes, I do. And I know he tried the same stunt on someone else."

"What an enterprising young man! Well, he was very charming on the telephone and wanted to come up from Adams and meet me. He asked what kind of flowers I liked best and I'm sure he was going to embark on a selection of chocolates to go with them. I almost continued to lead him on, but I knew I wouldn't have the heart to pull it off."

"What do you mean?"

"Theodore had the mumps as a young man and was not able to have children. That was a sticking point with both former wives, but it didn't bother me in the least. When I told the young man, his charming voice came to an abrupt halt, and he told me that couldn't be possible. His mother could confirm if there was any doubt. I very uncharitably suggested that perhaps his mother could come up with someone else to claim the honor of having him as a son and the reason why. He hung up on me."

We continued our game in silence, a game with which she was obviously well practiced as she outwitted me at every turn and unloaded the cards in her hand to win. Pauline came in with the tea and after she put it on the tray whispered to me, "They're here."

"Who's here?"

"The police," Pauline answered.

"What's happened?" Mrs. Schaeffer asked.

"Nothing's happened. The maids have all left, that's all," I said.

"Ah," Mrs. Schaeffer said. "I don't want to talk to the police just now."

"And Doctor Taylor."

"Pauline, will you hold them off for a bit?"

"Sure," she said and left the room.

I was still seated on the chair next to the bed while she fiddled with her tea. I dealt myself a hand of solitaire on the bedspread waiting for her to talk. But she said nothing.

"Who were they?" I asked.

"What?" she asked, all-innocent eyes large in her face.

"The six girls who came in disguise and flitted out of here today. What were they to you?"

"I hired them to come here to help out."

"With no housekeeper to supervise them? Very clever."

"I couldn't find one."

"I don't think so. I think you had things planned out very well. Did you find them, or did they find you?"

She took as deep a breath as she was able and paused. "They came to me. There were six of them and they had a familiar, sorry story to tell about my husband. They had worked for him in one of the fashion showrooms and he 'took liberties', as they politely say. Although his behavior was anything but polite. Lucky for him he had the mumps, or he would have had a truckload of children to support. Each girl vouched for the other, and I believed them. Why not? I was used to his crass behavior, and I knew about the rumors before we married." She stopped to take a deep breath. "I'm finding it harder to breathe," she stated, looking surprised.

"I know. I'm sorry." I decided to continue the story for her.

"So, you hatched a plan where you would persuade your husband to leave the City since he was being hounded by the press, former partners, ex-wives and, unknown to him and you at the time, the enterprising Otis Warren. Or whatever his name really is. I'll bet you suggested something like, 'Buy a house somewhere remote and I'll take care of hiring the staff and all the rest.' You figured something would happen and Theodore would die, perhaps out in the woods in a hunting accident or from a tumble down the stairs. And you would be a rich widow and live in peace."

"But then I got sick. Very badly. Very fast."

"So, the plan changed a little bit. Now you had to work against time. The girls, all young, pretty and slim, were outfitted to be drab, lumpy and unattractive in those dreadful wigs. Plop glasses on them, have them shuffle about and nobody from the outside, especially the cook who was closeted in the kitchen all day, would be able to tell one from the other. What you weren't expecting was that your husband would hire me to keep you company. Somebody who had full access to the house and might catch on that things here weren't what they seemed."

That elicited a smile from her.

"You've been lovely, but I hoped for someone a lot less observant," she said.

"Once you were stuck with me, why not take full advantage of the situation? You weren't able to hurl your husband down the stairs, but six healthy young women could hold him down and suffocate him with no problem."

She looked away but didn't say anything.

"And so he died. Not after I left that evening, but before I even got here, I think. That whole business about him stomping around in the hall, muttering to one of the maids, that same maid or another handing me the pay envelope that she said he gave her. All a charade. A nice touch was that someone had the idea to light a cigar so that when I went down the stairs at the end of my shift, I could believe he was in his study after his phone call. Aren't you lucky that I didn't think to stop by his study to thank him? I might have found a lit cigar in the ashtray, or perhaps one of the maids waving it around. In either case, that was a chance they took."

"You do have a lively imagination," she said.

"And the will. Interesting that you recently changed your will."

"Of course. Theodore was to inherit everything. Since his death, I had to make changes."

I smiled at her. "Let me guess: aside from some charities of which you are fond, there are likely six individuals, young women, who will share in the bounty."

She turned her head away. "I'm very tired. Could you call your husband? I believe I need another shot."

I patted her arm. "I'll get him. And I'll tell the police that you have nothing to say at this time. After all, you certainly weren't expecting the entire staff to leave so suddenly. With no forwarding addresses, I'm guessing?"

She managed a small smile and I left to see Inspector Gladstone.

Chapter 17

John went upstairs and I took Inspector Gladstone into the sitting room. Why not? No one in the house used it. Although I couldn't see Mount Greylock in the dark, just knowing it was there helped to settle my conflicting feelings. Gladstone was in an unusually calm mood and waited for me to talk.

"I don't think she has long," I said. "I should have asked her if she wanted to have Reverend Lewis come by for some words of comfort."

He looked at me closely, I took a deep breath and related what I thought had happened to Mr. Schaeffer and how.

"The maids are all gone?" he asked.

"Yes, they left quickly and who knows where they are right now. They pretended not to trust one another but that last episode of shouting was a charade. My guess is that they all worked for Mr. Schaeffer in the fashion showroom and had to put up with his advances or be out of a job. At least one of them was fired, from what I heard. I think one of them got up the nerve to approach Mrs. Schaeffer and the plan was hatched. Assemble those who had been most affected, fit them out as domestic workers, dress them alike, pad them out to make them unattractive, put wigs and glasses on them and, as far as Mrs. Schaeffer was concerned, that would put them out of danger.

The worse part was involving me as a bogus witness to the scheme by making it seem he was alive while I was in the house and some intruder had done the deed. What now?"

John had returned and stood in the doorway. "She's in a bad state. You might want to look in on her."

I got up to do so.

"I hate to admit defeat, but I don't know what we can do now," Gladstone said. "Nobody has admitted anything and six young women, whose real identities or even physical descriptions are a mystery, have skipped town. Where to? Who knows?" He stood up, looking resigned. "Thank you for your help," he said to me before he left.

Pauline was with her when I got up to the bedroom and Mrs. Schaeffer seemed to be asleep or at least not in pain.

"You've had quite a day," Pauline said. "I can stay with her."

"Thank you," I said with a sigh. "Call us if you need anything, but I will be back early in the morning."

Pauline took my arm. "She said something. Not to me, but almost to herself. 'If you seek revenge, dig two graves.'"

A chilling remark, but how like her to acknowledge her predicament. And it was prescient in that she passed away during the night, very peacefully. All alone in that big house, except for Pauline sitting next to the bed.

∼

IT WAS two days before Christmas that a familiar face appeared at the Adams office. Robert Sullivan, Mrs. Schaeffer's attorney, asked to speak to me in private. Although the will needed to go through probate and it would take some time, he informed me that she had made a sizable bequest to me.

'For your kindness and forgiveness,' is what she wrote.

My eyes welled with tears at the thought of her sad end at such a young age. "Were there any other recipients?" I asked.

"Oh, yes. The sale of Highfields will provide funds for some of her favorite charities." He paused, knowing I waited for more. "And there were some young women who she thought needed additional assistance and they have been provided for handsomely."

We looked at one another and I wondered how much he knew or suspected.

"I'll be in touch," he said kindly as he left.

"What was that about?" John asked as the door closed behind the attorney.

"It seems Christmas has come a bit early for us. Not in the way I wanted it to, but the way someone else planned it." I hugged him tightly because I couldn't think of anything else to say.

~

We've met cousin Amanda Burnside in MURDER AT THE VALENTINE BALL and MURDER AT THE BEACH HOUSE.

NOW SHE'S GOT a series of her own, MASSACHUSETTS COZY MYSTERIES, that take place in Boston in the early 1930s. Amanda turns sleuth and faces upper class Boston Brahmin, feisty newcomers, gangsters, bootleggers, politicians and a handsome Irish detective.

Find it here:

ANDREA KRESS

MURDER ON BOSTON COMMON
Check out my website for more titles.
www.Andreas-books.com
See the entire series:
Berkshires Cozy Mysteries

Thank you! Happy Reading,
Andrea

Printed in Great Britain
by Amazon